én•nēad:
A group of nine

ABOUT THE AUTHOR

Lisa Heidle writes flash, short and long form fiction, articles and book reviews. Her work has appeared in Sabal Literary Journal, Mash Stories, Second Hand Stories, The Chattahoochee Review, the Flash Fiction Magazine Anthology and other literary journals. This is her first collection of short stories.

én•nēad

stories by
Lisa Heidle

FOR MY MOTHER,

PAMELA ELAINE MASON

1949-2012

CONTENT

Foreword

Foreword

The short story, as a medium in literature, has often carried with it a reputation as varied as the subject matter it has brought to life. While I am in no way going to unpack that spectrum of opinion here, I would like to briefly share with you, dear reader, some humble thoughts that my co-conspirators at The Two Keys Press and I have on this aforementioned format.

We believe that the short story as an art form is a powerful vehicle to relay important ideas and experiences, both fictional and factual. It is not practice for a novel or primarily part of a bigger thing; it is the thing itself. And in a society that is cultivating a progressively shorter attention span, the short story is perhaps more relevant today than it has ever been. America has an incredibly rich history of short story writing and it is with this heritage in mind that we now bring to you the short stories of Lisa Heidle.

If you met her in a coffee shop, you would never suspect Lisa Heidle of being the author of such an unsettling collection of narratives. It is a minor observation that highlights the insight the author possesses into human nature and circumstances incredibly unlike her own. Heidle has the uncanny ability to take us behind the curtain of seemingly bizarre, sensational, and disturbing events to subtly reveal genuine motivations and emotions in a way that humanizes characters that might otherwise live only as local gossip or newspaper headlines.

The inherent power of the short story lies in its brevity. It allows the author to take the reader from the induction to the completion of an intentional atmosphere without an inevitable break in the enchantment that would occur with long form literature. It is with this idea in mind that we invite you to immerse yourself in these stories by reading each of them in a single sitting. The strength of these works is most apparent when a constant steeping of language has produced a mind that is fully enveloped in the intended mood.

It is our sincere hope that you will find your mind expanded by the art of Lisa Heidle.

Trey Penton
Creative Director
The Two Keys Press

A Myriad of Responses

I went to work for the Trasks after the pancreatic cancer had taken up residence and refused to move on from the couple's two-story house. For a hospice worker, it was a relatively easy assignment. I took care of the 44-year-old Mrs. Trask during the day: helped her eat, administered pain meds, kept her company. When Mr. Trask came home from work, I went back to my place and worked on my novel, a science-fiction thriller that'd been my main focus, the hub of my existence, what my friends' called Jack's opus, for the last decade of my life.

The first day I met my new ward, Mr. Trask and I spoke in the kitchen. He told me the diagnosis, the medications his wife took, the prognosis. The hospice workers were given all the pertinent information, but I let the man speak, knowing that having something to share gave the loved ones a feeling of control in an out-of-control situation.

"They did two rounds of Gemzar. She decided not to try again. She couldn't function. Not that she functions much now, mostly reads and sleeps. She loves smashed bananas in the morning. It's one of the only things she still wants to eat. And if you do laundry, don't use the dryer sheets, they give her a rash," Mr. Trask said with a look of confusion over the raised blisters that peppered his wife's skin. "I don't know why, they didn't use to."

The man's eyes were shot through with red and dry flakes coated his hairline and shirt collar. Stress-induced psoriasis. I'd seen it on many of the caregivers. In my notebook, I jotted down a reminder to bring a topical ointment the next time I came.

"Why don't I introduce the two of you? Of course she gets the last say. I'm sure she'll like you. Carla likes everyone, she's never met a stranger. And she'll be a perfect patient. She never complains."

In my ten years of doing in-home care, I'd found that no two people handled the experience of dying the same. Some, wanting friends and family to remember them as strong and brave, chose stoicism in the face of the inevitable. Others raged against the injustice, making sure that those closest to them understood that what was happening was wrong and under no circumstance to be condoned. The hardest ones for me to work with were those who wore naked fear on their face, blinking rapidly and wringing their dry, paper-thin hands, unable to untie the complicated knot that had become their life. For the dying, there was a myriad of responses.

"Assuming you know another's pain and fear is like saying you know their thoughts. Not possible," Dot, my hospice leader, shared with the class on the first day of training. "Your job is to make them comfortable and anticipate their needs. Dying is a solitary occupation, no matter who's in the room."

At the time, I considered her cold and unfeeling, promising myself I'd never become so jaded. Over the years, I'd adopted the belief and repeated it as my own.

Mr. Trask led me through the living room toward the front of the house.

"We had to move our bedroom down here when the stairs became too much. They're pretty steep. When we bought the place, we used to joke about putting in an elevator so we wouldn't have to climb them."

We entered what had once been the dining area. The table had been replaced with a hospital bed and a dresser with a television centered on top. An unmade futon where Mr. Trask slept lounged beneath the picture window and a large china cabinet sat in the corner; orange pill bottles, blankets and books filled the shelves where plates, teacups and saucers should have been.

"Honey, this is Jack, he's going to be helping us out. Jack, this is Mrs. Trask."

I took her hand in mine, careful not to apply too much pressure. Chemo could weaken bones, make them brittle. A few years before, I'd assisted a fifty-year-old man struggling with the same cancer as Mrs. Trask whose wrist snapped when his son tried to climb onto his lap. I could still hear the sound of bone separating from bone.

Mrs. Trask's handshake was still strong. "It's nice to meet you. Please, call me Carla."

Her green eyes surrounded by jaundiced whites held mine. I felt as if she was looking through me, could see my life from the moment of birth: my first word, first bike, first love. The first time my mother packed her clothes to leave and I begged her to stay, crying and pulling on the sweater coat she wore. The last time she came back and I refused to speak until she smacked me in the mouth and called me selfish. The ankle I sprained in second grade playing Red Rover; the car I wrecked on the way to the prom; the night I left Amy Freeman behind at a Bon Jovi concert because her best friend promised to let me go all the way, then only let me slide my fingers inside her bra.

The night my mother died and I cried so long and so hard my nose bled.

When Carla pulled her gaze away, it felt as if I'd been startled from a deep, dream-filled sleep.

I arrived at the Trask home at six the next morning. Mr. Trask met me at the front door, shoes in one hand, briefcase in the other.

"She had a rough night," he said in a whisper, the dark circles under his eyes saying that his wife wasn't alone in her struggle. "She's sleeping now, try not to wake her." He sat down on the front porch steps and pulled on his shoes. "Call my cell if you need anything." He hurried to the garage, eyes on his feet, briefcase gripped tight to his chest.

I opened the front door and listened to the sounds of a slumbering home filled with death. It always sounded the same: a low-level hum of denial that only the most discerning ear could hear.

"Tim?" Carla called out for her husband.

"He left. But I'm here," I said as I entered the room. "Do you need something?"

"I need to go to the restroom. Can you help me?"

"Would it be easier to use the bedpan?"

"I prefer to do it the old-fashioned way," she said, dropping one leg over the side of the bed, followed by the second.

"If you want to go old school, I can take you outside and let you squat in the weeds." The words left my mouth before I thought them through. I started to apologize. The smile on my patient's face told me there was no need.

"I think we'll do it this way for now. After we get to know one another better, then we can take a day trip."

*

Over the next six weeks, I did my best to ease Carla's pain and keep her firmly planted in the land of the living. Some days were easier than others. When the pain receded, Carla would talk about the books she loved and her fifth-grade students from her twenty years of teaching. We would talk about my novel and she would tell me how wonderful it was, even though she'd never read a word. We watched old movies, both sharing a love for noir films from the fifties. Her favorite was Orson Welles' *Touch of Evil*. "It's everything people try to deny about themselves, all the ugly that lives just below the surface. It gives you permission not to try so hard to be good."

Days when the pain clawed its way to the surface, the hours would pass slowly, each minute stretching out until the next round of pain medication could be given.

Pleasure mixed with shame would course through me when Carla called out my name when waking, asking if it was time for more.

After going home to my apartment, I would wake, thinking I'd heard her. The next morning, I would speed across town in the cold dawn, the sharp snap of frozen grass beneath my feet as I rushed across the Trask lawn. I'd allow Mr. Trask to update me on the previous night, itching to get inside and take up what I considered my calling.

*

Carla was a private woman—closing the door after I helped her into the bathroom and asking me to leave the room when she gave herself a sponge bath after standing in the shower had become too tiring. The day she asked to use the bedpan, I knew we'd turned a corner and were never coming back. She tugged her nightgown up around her waist. I helped lift her hips, the bones protruding beneath white skin, her abdomen bloated and tender, and slipped the bedpan beneath her.

"Would you like me to step out?" I asked.

"I no longer have any secrets from you, Jackie-boy."

"My mother used to call me that," I mumbled.

"Really? Mine just called me an inconvenience."

The bitterness in Carla's voice shocked me. Even during the worst of the discomfort, she'd only had kindness in her words.

"Are you in a lot of pain?" I asked.

"No more than usual. Why?"

"No reason. Are you finished?"

"Yeah. I'm really tired this morning. I'll have my bananas when I wake up."

I removed the waste and carried it to the bathroom. Closing the door behind me, I hesitated before dumping the dark yellow urine into the toilet. I took a breath. It was there, the rich odor of death. My tears dripped into the golden liquid like coins into a pond. Whispering a quick wish, I tipped the pan and watched the urine splash into the clear water.

*

The next two weeks showed a marked downturn. Carla was unable to get out of bed or stay awake for any length of time. I sat by her side, trying to watch movies, but mostly watching her as she slept the deep sleep of someone slipping from the world. I took note of the turned up nose and the soft down of hair on her face that had sprouted when she stopped chemo. It took all my willpower not to climb into the bed, pull her close and hold on tight, be a tether to a life I wanted her to keep.

Mr. Trask started coming home later and later, something I'd seen before. In my experience, most men tended to avoid the issue, whereas, when the roles were reversed—a woman caring for a man—she'd put all of her life away: job, friends, other family members became secondary to the time and attention shown to the failing loved one.

When Carla would wake and ask in a dry, raspy voice, "Is Tim home yet?" anger flooded through me, making my hands shake as I lifted a glass of water to her cracked lips.

"Not yet. Soon," was my pat answer.

The day the pain was the worst, untouchable by the medication, and Carla moaned and writhed against the sickness that had invaded her body, I met her husband at the front door. He was two hours late. I closed the door quietly behind me as I stepped onto the porch.

"Is everything okay?" Mr. Trask asked. Fear for the response was thick in his voice. I chose to ignore it.

"She asked for you all day."

"Things at work have been crazy."

He tried to move past me. I held my ground.

"She needs you."

"I know."

"No, you don't. Or you wouldn't be getting home so late."

"You'll be paid for your time."

"I'm not worried about the money. It's her I'm concerned about."

A Myriad of Responses

I noticed that Mr. Trask's psoriasis was gone and had been replaced with a look of contentment. A strange look for a husband whose wife lay dying twenty-feet away. I took a step closer and sniffed—perfume overlaying a thicker, musky odor.

"She's dying," I said through clenched teeth.

"I know that."

We kept our voices at a whisper so Carla wouldn't hear.

"How can you treat her like this?"

"What business is it of yours?"

"I care about her. She's a wonderful woman."

"And a dying woman. You said so yourself."

"She needs you," I repeated. Carla wanted him by her side and even though it pained me to know that she wanted another man more than me, especially one undeserving of her love, I was going to see she got what she wanted.

"Carla only needs her morphine. And you," Mr. Trask said, followed by a snort of derision.

"You don't deserve her."

"Probably not. But I had her. Can you say as much?"

My face flamed, knowing that my charge's husband knew my deep want for his wounded wife.

Before I could reply, Carla called out.

"She wants you," I mumbled as I walked down the front steps toward my car. "I'll be back in the morning."

I lay awake that night listening to the traffic from the interstate, so different from the suburban sounds of children and garage doors I heard during the day in the Trask neighborhood. I prayed, something I hadn't done since my mother passed. I wasn't sure if I was praying for Carla to live or to die. One was selfish and one wasn't; I'd lost the ability to tell the difference.

*

Mr. Trask waited for me on the porch the next morning. The high color on his cheeks from the night before was gone. His skin was sallow and his lips looked as dry as Carla's. He spoke without looking me in the eye. "We had a hard night. A lot to discuss. I'm going to take a half day. I'll be back after lunch."

"I'll call if there's a change."

"We want to thank you for all you've done." Mr. Trask stared out across the lawn as if he was looking into his future and couldn't see anything familiar. "We. I won't be saying that much longer, will I?"

Carla was sitting up in bed, dressed in a sheer white nightgown that I'd never seen. I blushed and tried not to stare.

"Is that new?"

"It was tucked in the bottom of a drawer. Tim found it."

"You look lovely."

"Thank you, kind sir. I have a little more energy today and the pain isn't as bad as yesterday. I want to do something, but I need your help."

Carla asked me to carry her upstairs to the bedroom she'd shared with her husband. "I need to put my affairs in order. Isn't that what they call it?" she asked as I disconnected the IV line and lifted her from the bed.

"I believe so."

"Maybe my husband should do the same."

She wrapped her arms around my neck and rested her head against my chest. Pulling her close, I marveled at her lightness, enjoying the feel of her in my arms.

We took the steep stairs slowly.

A Myriad of Responses

"Our room is at the end of the hall. I haven't been up here for so long I can't remember what it looks like."

The room was chilly compared to the rest of the house and smelled musty. I carried her to a chaise lounge in the corner and she covered herself with a teal throw that was draped over the back.

"I forgot I had this. When I bought it, I loved it. Had to have it. Then I forgot about it. Isn't life strange?" she said, burying her face in the soft material. "We need to go through my clothes. We're going to choose two outfits, one for the viewing and one for the burial."

I looked away so she couldn't see the tears in my eyes. "Why two?"

"Because I refuse to be buried in anything other than jeans and a t-shirt. Eternity's a long time and I want to be comfortable."

She chose a red blouse and gray slacks for the viewing.

"The red will pull out the green in your eyes," I said.

Carla laughed. "I don't think anyone's going to see my eyes. What do you think about this?" She held up a purple tee with *Reading Is Sexy* written across the front.

"I think it's perfect."

We spent the next few hours going through drawers and placing items into three piles: Distribute to friends and family. Give to charity. Keep for Tim.

"This should make it easier for him," Carla said when we closed the last box.

"Are you ready to go back down?" I asked.

"There's one more thing I want to do."

"What's that?"

Carla pulled her nightgown over her head and leaned back.

"Are you hot?" I asked, confused. I wanted to look away but couldn't pull my eyes from her.

"Come here."

I did what she said, my breath heavy, sweat breaking out on my forehead. She pulled me towards her. I stopped my fall on the arm of the lounge. "I might hurt you."

"Then be careful. And go slow," she said before kissing me.

When it was over and we lay on the chaise, I fought to find the courage to ask the question that had tumbled through my head as I explored her ailing body, ran my hands over her soft newly-grown hair, convincing myself that the grimaces and groans were from pleasure, not pain.

"Why?"

She shrugged. "Why not?"

I didn't push the issue.

"We'd better hurry. Tim will be home soon," Carla said, trying to stand. "Help me."

Carla held her arms up over her head like a child and I redressed her in the nightgown. I lifted her back into my arms and carried her to the top of the stairs.

"Put me down."

I did what she asked, keeping one arm around her waist.

"Are you ready?" she asked, looking up at me.

"For what?"

"To let me go."

"I never want to let you go. I love you," I said, unembarrassed, realizing that the truth left no room for shame.

"I don't mean figuratively let me go. I mean literally. Let me go."

It took me a minute to realize what she was asking. "No," I said, gripping her tight.

"It's time."

"No."

"If you love me like you just said, you'll do it. Tell Tim that you left me upstairs to get more boxes, I made my way to the stairs and fell."

"No." I started to cry, a wet sound that came from some deep part of me that I didn't know existed.

"Please, Jackie-boy. I need you to do this."

"I can't."

"You're the only one who can."

I tried to lift her back into my arms. She pushed me away. "Stop. This is what I want. Do it."

"It's not right."

"None of this is right. Don't make me tell you all the reasons I need you to do it. The word for how wrong all of this is hasn't been created yet." She pulled me to her and kissed me again. I tasted blood on her broken lips.

Carla stepped away. I let her. She stood in the center of the top stair, arms at her sides, hands gripping the creamy material of the nightgown, looking back at me. "Do it."

Standing behind her, I laid my hands on her shoulders. I could feel her bones protruding under the skin and her body's heat on my palms.

I kissed the nape of her neck, the new hairs soft on my lips, and pushed hard.

She fell, her hands still holding tight to the gown I'd only moments before slipped over her arms, down her body. I covered my ears, hoping to muffle the sound of her hitting the steps. The snapping of her fragile bones sounded loud in the quiet of the house.

Before calling the ambulance and Mr. Trask, I cradled the misshapen head of the woman I loved and looked into her eyes. It felt like they were looking through me, could see my life from the moment of birth.

Closure

Bitsy Douglas took the train from Poughkeepsie to Manhattan alone for the first time in her twenty-two years. Convincing her mother to let her come into the city without an escort wasn't easy, especially so close to the wedding.

"It's 1962, Mother, not 1862," Bitsy mumbled at her steak tartare, an uncooked slab of beef that always made her grind her teeth and swallow hard.

The comment incited a lecture on the importance of appearance, regardless of the date on the calendar. When her mother had exhausted her arsenal of all the reasons Bitsy shouldn't go—rape, murder, foreigners—she capitulated. *Only two days, Elizabeth. Any longer and it's possible you'll be debased.*

She hoped two days would be enough time to heal from the procedure. Pressing her legs together, she squirmed in her seat and tried not to imagine what was going to be done down there—*the place good girls never touch*—by a man she didn't know.

Bitsy took the receipt from Doyle's Café out of her pocketbook and read the address written across the back. Her best friend, Dot, had driven her across the river to an old diner in Clintondale. A hard looking woman named Nell flipped a receipt over and wrote: 274 Terris Place, Suite 200. She made Bitsy memorize the doctor's name.

"Be careful who you tell about this," Nell said. "If the wrong person finds out, it could ruin it for the others. Understand?"

Bitsy nodded and tucked the receipt into her coat pocket where she kept it gripped tight until she was home. She hurried to the pink and apple green bedroom she'd had all her life, closed and locked the door, taking the extra precaution of wedging the back of her desk chair beneath the doorknob. The ink was smudged from her moist palm, but was still readable. Redemption danced between each word, offering hope.

"Two seventy-four Terris Place, please," she told the driver, ignoring the smell of sweat that filled the cab. Her mother would've insisted the driver roll down a window or that they change cars.

"Do you mean Terris Street?" the driver asked.

"No, it's Terris Place. At least I think that's the right address," Bitsy said. She slipped the receipt from her pocketbook, glanced at it, then shoved it back into her bag.

"It's Terris Place," she said with more certainty than she felt.

"You know that's in the Jewish quarter, don't you?"

"Is that a problem?" She turned her full gaze on the driver and gave him the look her mother gave the caterer when she felt he was trying to overcharge for salmon puffs.

"Not for me, Miss. A fare's a fare."

Bitsy watched the tall buildings tick past and let her mind wander to Keith. She met him at a party Dot and the other girls from the sorority had dragged her to on the Harvard campus. She assumed he went there. He never corrected her. She liked that he didn't cut his dark curly hair short like the other boys. When he looked at her, there was a gentle tug in her center. She thought it was love.

They dated for a month before she gave in to the urgency she felt when parked in the dark, secluded areas Keith always seemed to find. After the uncomfortable first time, the subsequent encounters were thrilling. Bitsy blushed when thinking about the whoops, moans and repeated words of gratitude offered up to God that filled Keith's old 1953 Studebaker.

Within a short time, she'd become quite adept at the one thing she'd overheard her mother describe to the Bridge Club ladies as *a woman's burden and duty*.

After a few months, Keith started to change. Regular phone calls became sporadic, dates cancelled, and the ones he didn't cancel, he showed up for hours late, offering no excuse other than he had things to do. It was Dot who exposed him. She found Keith working in his father's garage two towns over. Her friend asked around the little town and learned he'd never attended Harvard and had dropped out of school the day he turned fifteen. Sitting across the street from the garage, they watched Keith work, his hands covered in grease.

"Didn't you notice his fingernails?" Dot asked.

"He told me he was a painter. He was going to paint my portrait."

When Keith closed the large metal garage door and turned off the open sign, Bitsy crossed the street and confronted him.

He didn't look surprised to see her. When she asked him why he did what he did, he shrugged and said it was fun while it lasted. "Didn't you have a good time?" he asked. Bitsy slapped him.

A girl approached them, pushing a baby carriage.

"Who's this, Keith?" she asked, looking Bitsy up and down.

"No one," he mumbled.

"Who are you?" Bitsy asked, wiping the tears from her face.

"Rita. His wife."

Bitsy walked back to the car. She refused to speak about Keith again. She didn't have the words to express the pain and didn't want to diminish it by trying.

After graduation, she moved back home. When her mother grew frustrated with her sleeping ten hours a day—*idleness is unappealing, Elizabeth*—she forced her to go on a date with the son of a family friend. Six months later, Beau asked her to marry him. Bitsy said she would in the same way she would've agreed to attend a formal at the country club. Beau didn't seem to notice her listless response. In the quiet moments, when no one was asking her opinion on linens or flower arrangements, she questioned why she'd said yes to Beau. He wasn't Keith was the only answer she could come up with, the only answer that felt right. And that was good enough to last her a lifetime. At least she hoped it would be.

"Here we are, Terris Place," the cab driver said, sweeping his hand at the old brownstone like he was trying to sell it.

"Are you sure this is right?" Bitsy asked.

"It's what you said. Do you want me to wait?"

Closure

She told him no, gathered her things and stepped out of the car. People pushed past without an apology, something her mother would've found crass. She saw a diner sign down the block. Waiting for a break in the flow, she stepped in and let it take her where she needed to go.

Bitsy entered the half-filled diner. Stainless steel counter and red booths. Garlic and a vinegary, sweet smell in the air. Self-conscious, she hurried to a small table by the window that gave a full view of the diner and the sidewalk.

A waitress handed her a menu. "Welcome to Rachmann's. Today's special is stuffed cabbage. What can I get you?"

Bitsy read the menu. Fried keplach. Kishka. Matzo brie. "I'll take the special," she said. "And an iced tea."

"I'll have that right out."

Bitsy tried not to stare at the men dressed in black suits, white shirts and large black hats. They had long ringlets, one on each side. The curls reminded her of the ones she wore when she was young. Being born with stick straight hair was Bitsy's first affront to her mother, a slight the woman demanded be righted by the nanny who placed curlers in her hair as soon as it was long enough to be wound around the hard plastic. Bitsy's scalp still ached when she thought about the long nights spent trying to sleep on her stomach, fighting to keep her face out of the pillow.

The waitress brought the food with a basket of rolls. Bitsy ate until the plate was clean. Her mother would've been appalled, believing that a true lady eats just enough not to insult the chef and never eats a full meal when she's with the opposite sex. *Men do not want to see a woman behaving in animalistic behaviors, Elizabeth. It's unseemly.*

"You must've been hungry," the waitress said with a smile.

"It was delicious."

"Would you like a slice of pie?"

"Maybe in a little while."

The diner started to empty, leaving a handful of customers reading newspapers and sipping coffee. One man caught her attention in the way he turned the pages of the paper carefully, as if not wanting to wrinkle them. He had ringlets like the other men. His were short and dark. Bitsy imagined running her fingers through the tight curls and letting them spring back into place. He looked up and smiled. She felt the familiar tug in her center and looked away.

After motioning for a refill on her iced tea, she took out her notebook and scanned the items still needed for the wedding and honeymoon. Thank you gifts for the bridesmaids topped the list. Her mother wanted to give strings of pearls. Bitsy insisted on wristwatches for the four women in the wedding party. In showing her disapproval, believing a wristwatch on a woman to be gauche, Mrs. Douglas refused to purchase them.

Bitsy had bought Beau a set of golf clubs he'd had his eyes on. He worked for his father's insurance company and played golf at the club on the weekends. He was honest and reliable, even if he was a bit dull. And he respected her. When they went to the movies, he held her hand, and when they necked, he always showed restraint, stopping even when she didn't want to. The night he proposed, he said he would wait for her forever, but hoped it wouldn't be that long. Those words, coupled with the look of disgust whenever he heard of a woman who'd "given herself away" had forced her to come to the city. He'd made his expectations for his new bride clear.

Chewing her bottom lip, she imagined what her life would be like if Beau found out the truth. A bleak future living with her mother, attending garden club meetings and Thursday afternoon Bridge, constant complaining coupled with weekly visits to the salon was all she could see.

The waitress came back to the table. "Ready for pie?"

"What kind do you have?"

"The Nesselrode pie here is famous."

"I'll try it," Bitsy said.

It's a day of firsts, she decided. Maybe she would make it a practice, being daring and trying new things. She decided that she'd be more adventurous. Keith flashed through her mind.

"Maybe I'll be a cautious-adventurer," she mumbled to herself.

"What was that, Sweetheart?" the waitress asked as she placed the slice of pie on the table.

Blushing, Bitsy shook her head.

The first bite of custard topped with whipped cream and the pieces of candied fruit made her moan. It reminded her of when she was young and, after the house was quiet, she would sneak into the kitchen and eat vanilla pudding from the bowl, careful to smooth away her finger marks so the cook wouldn't know.

"Excuse me." The man who'd smiled at her earlier was standing so close she could've reached out and touched his thick wool pants. "I noticed how much you enjoyed the pie." His voice was soft and strong and Bitsy had to pull her gaze away from the deep brown eyes.

"It was delicious."

"My aunt does the baking here. The Nesselrode is her specialty. I'll tell her you enjoyed it."

"Please do."

"My name is Ephram." He held out his hand. It was warm, enveloping hers so completely that she imagined crawling in after it. Bitsy pulled her hand away and tucked it under her leg.

"I'm Elizabeth." She wasn't sure why she gave her full name. No one other than her mother called her that.

"It's nice to meet you, Elizabeth. I'll share your compliments with my aunt."

Bitsy watched Ephram leave the diner and cross the street. He disappeared into the mass of people, making her wonder if she'd conjured him. An adult imaginary friend. *Don't be frivolous, Elizabeth. Real life doesn't support such fancies of the mind.*

The cracked glass on the door of the brownstone rattled in the frame when it closed behind her. Bitsy's heart sank at the sight of the empty lobby. She didn't think she had enough strength to start over. Or time. The wedding was in two months.

"Miss? Can I help you?" a voice asked from behind her. A woman sat at a small desk tucked into the corner.

"I'm looking for Dr. Tomlin's office," she said, not making eye contact.

"Dr. Tomlin is on the second floor. The elevators are straight ahead and the doctor's office is the third door on your right."

The elevator creaked its way to the second floor, opening to a dim hallway that smelled of damp carpet and disinfectant.

Closure

Bitsy stopped in front of the door with Dr. Samuel Tomlin in bold black letters, took a deep breath, and opened it.

There were five women, three about her age, two older, in the waiting room. She'd hoped no one else would be there, then realized how silly it was to think she was the only person with such a problem.

"May I help you?" a woman asked from behind a glass partition.

"I have an appointment at two with Dr. Tomlin."

"Name?"

"Bitsy Douglas. Or Elizabeth. I can't remember which name I used."

"We have you here as Bitsy. Have a seat and we'll call you when the doctor is ready."

She sat in-between one of the older women and a younger one.

"I'm Kelly," the younger woman next to her said. "My appointment isn't until three. I decided to come early. Nervous energy, I suppose."

"There's no need to worry," the woman on the other side of Bitsy said. "There's nothing to it. I've had it done twice."

Before Bitsy could ask why anyone would need it done more than once, the nurse called the older woman's name and motioned for her to come into the back.

Kelly was a talker. Bitsy nodded and let her ramble on about her upcoming wedding and where she was going on her honeymoon. Just as Kelly was launching into the reason behind choosing lavender bridesmaid dresses over robin's egg blue, the nurse opened the door and motioned for Bitsy.

"You can leave your suitcase with me. I'll keep it here at the front desk," the nurse said.

She hadn't been aware of how tight she'd been gripping the handle until the nurse took it away.

Bitsy followed her down the hallway and into a small room on the right.

"Here's a gown. You don't need to take off your top, just your bottoms. The doctor will be administering a local anesthetic."

"Like the dentist?"

The nurse laughed. "A little different, but the same idea. It's to numb the area. Any other questions?"

"I don't think so."

"The doctor will be in soon," she said as she left.

With shaking hands, Bitsy removed her jacket, folding and laying it over the back of a chair. She unbuttoned her skirt and stepped out of it along with her slip. Sitting in the chair, she removed her stockings, careful not to tear the fine material. She slipped off her panties and tucked them between her skirt and slip.

She wrapped the gown tight and hopped up on the examination table. The room was chilly and she wished she'd left her suit jacket on.

The man she'd spoken with at the diner came into the room.

"Hello again," he said. "Elizabeth, right?"

"Or Bitsy. I go by both." Bitsy's voice was unusually high. "I thought you said your name was Ephram?"

"My uncle is Dr. Tomlin. We share the practice."

"Is he here?" The idea of having the man with the rich brown eyes see her in such a private way was more than she could stand.

"I'm afraid he's with another patient. Don't worry, I've done this many times."

"I don't think I want to do this," Bitsy said, trying to get off the table without the gown falling open.

"Please, sit down," Ephram said, pulling a stool from the corner and sitting in front of her. "Let's talk for a moment." He clasped her hands in one of his own. "Tell me why you've changed your mind."

"I don't know," she said, trying not to cry.

"Do I make you uncomfortable?"

Bitsy's manners wouldn't allow her to say yes, so she said nothing.

"Let me tell you a little about myself, maybe that'll help put you at ease. I've been working with my uncle for the past five years and I'm to be married this fall. Now tell me about you."

"I went to Wellesley and I'm getting married in eight weeks."

"Congratulations. Is that why you're here?"

Bitsy nodded.

"Planning a wedding is stressful. At least that's what my fiancée keeps telling me," Ephram said.

"My mother is doing most of it. She even planned our honeymoon."

Ephram laughed. "My mother would do the same if I let her. The procedure we're going to do today is simple and should be healed by your wedding night. Are you ready to proceed?"

"I don't know."

"Do you have more questions?"

Stalling for time, Bitsy asked, "Why do you do this?"

"Why did I become a doctor?"

"No. This. What I want done."

"It's not all I do." Ephram hesitated. "I think it's important."

"Why?" *It's rude to delve into someone's personal choices, Elizabeth.*

He patted her leg. "Lie back and I'll tell you while we get started."

Bitsy laid down and focused on the large water stain above her that looked like a continent.

"Put your feet in here and let your knees fall apart. Good. Try to stop shaking. There you go. Now you're going to feel a sharp prick as I administer the anesthetic. Okay, we'll give it a minute to start working. I decided to do this because of my sister, Esther. She was a few years older than me. She was funny and intelligent and had a kind heart. Now I'm going to make the incision and start the stitching. You'll feel some slight tugging, but shouldn't feel any pain. Can you feel that?"

"A little. It doesn't hurt."

"I'm using an interrupted stitch. Don't startle when you hear the scissors clipping the thread. Esther went away to school and when she returned, our father decided it was time for her to marry. We grew up knowing that our marriages would be arranged, but it still took her by surprise. Since Father had let her go away to school, she thought he would let her choose her husband. I was the only one she told about her college boyfriend. They'd broken it off after graduation. Just two more stitches and we're done. As the wedding day moved closer, Esther became more desperate, knowing that on her wedding night, her husband would know she'd been with another man." Ephram paused, then added, "It was too much for her. She took her life. I decided that no other woman should ever feel like there are no choices."

The silence was heavy in the room. Bitsy tried to find the words that would let Ephram know she understood how

Esther had felt. She didn't know how to explain the fear of being called a fraud.

Ephram reappeared from between her legs. "There we go, all done. You can sit up now."

"That's it?"

"That's it. In six weeks, come back and we'll remove the stitches. Or go to your regular doctor."

There was no way old Dr. Belk, the same man who'd treated her for chicken pox and ear infections, would understand why she'd done such a thing. "I'll come back. Will my fiancé know?"

"Not unless you tell him."

"What about blood?"

"Some women experience slight tearing and pain, so be prepared. There should be a little blood. For all intents and purposes, you will be a virgin for your new groom."

Ephram left the room.

Bitsy waited until she was sure he wouldn't be returning before reaching between her legs. *Don't touch yourself, Elizabeth. Men don't like women who are improper with their person.* With shaking fingers, she traced the thick thread that held her together, bound her. Made her new.

A Broken Prayer

First appeared in Sabal Literary Journal, Vol. 10

Our Father, who art in heaven...

Me and Frank had You in our lives from the very beginning. In all your wisdom, You brought us together at Bible study with Reverend Thompson's wife. She had a soft spot in her heart for children, on the account of never having any of her own. My daddy said the reason the Thompsons never had any babies was because Reverend Thompson wasn't able to perform his manly duties. At the time, I didn't have the understanding of what he meant. Now that I know, I feel real bad for them and don't find any humor in their situation. My daddy could be a very crude man when he wanted to be.

hallowed be thy name...

Please forgive me for rambling on so. I have a tendency to do that and, as You know, it's gotten me into some pickles in my day. As I said, Frank and I met at Bible study. It wasn't a romantic sort of meeting. I noticed Frank, not because he was handsome or charming, but because he was the first man ever to look at me like I was worth being looked at. Maybe others need more, but that was enough for me. I've always been of the mind that life is hard and two can deal with it better than one.

The thing I remember most about Frank from when we were kids is the pig manure. It clung to his boots and you could see how he tried to scrape it off the best he could. That stuff is like cement once it attaches to something. None of the other girls wanted anything to do with him because of it, but I could see how embarrassed he was about the odor and how he held his head up just the same. Not the stuff those Turner Classic movies are made of, but that's how You brought me and my Frank together so many years ago.

Thy Kingdom come...
After marrying, we moved to town. We didn't have the money to buy any farmland and, truth be told, we'd both had enough of farming. For most, it's a hateful way of living and we didn't harbor any ideas that we were special enough to make a go of it, so we came out of the woods. I had eight years of schooling under my belt, which was pretty good for a girl of the time. Frank only had four because his daddy had to pull him out to help on the farm. It was a common thing to do back in the day.

It wasn't easy when we first moved in. Frank did odd jobs and I took in washing. Then Frank got on at Harper's Shoe Factory. We thanked You every day for sending him that job. It kept us going for many a year and being that Frank was never afraid of hard work, he did just fine there, even became a foreman. He retired four years ago. We were raised not to boast, but I could tell how touched he was when he got that plaque showing his years of service and that gold pen with his name on it. He never had nothing so nice. Harpers threw him a party and brought in a big sheet cake. It was store bought. I could've made one for half the price and it would've been twice as good to boot, but I didn't say nothing. It wouldn't of been right. I felt a bit out of place at Frank's work, but it was exciting just the same. I enjoyed seeing where he'd gone every morning at the crack of dawn for the past forty odd years. It was a very fine experience, I must tell You.

Even Hank came. I was worried he might try and ruin it somehow, but he behaved just fine. He wore his uniform and everyone commented on how handsome he was and how proud we must be. We smiled like we always do, because we are proud, but if we hadn't, Hank would of been sore. We didn't want to ruin the day by upsetting him.

Thy will be done...
You gave us our first baby about a year after Frank started at the factory. The doctor said he was too small and he only lived nine days. We were heartbroken. I still miss that little baby. I never knew a person could love another being that much. I was angry with You for a time after that. Then I came to understand that You have your reasons and they will be revealed to us all one day when we reach your Kingdom.

We tried for years after, but couldn't make another baby. It was such a hard time for the both of us. We so wanted a big family. Then lo and behold, I was looking at thirty-five candles on the cake and I was with child. I'll never forget the look on Frank's face when I told him. He went out and bought me a cross necklace, real 14-karate gold. I only wore it on Sundays when we attended church services. It was the only time Frank ever bought me something other than an appliance for the household. I still tear up when I think about that necklace and how much it meant to Frank to give it to me. We had so much hope then. I've learned that a person better watch what they hope for and be ready for everything that comes with the hoping. The good and the bad.

On earth as it is in heaven...

Hank was born a difficult child. Nothing ever seemed to please him. If I ran him a bath, it was too hot. If I added cold, it was too cold. They say that every child is born with a clean slate and anything that happens to make him bad is done after his birth. I don't believe that. You already had something scribbled down for our Hank, that much I know. I wonder at times if we'd done things different, like spanked him maybe, if we could've changed him. You say in your Good Book that if we spare the rod, we spoil the child, but I'd grown up on the wrong side of the belt and didn't want my child to fear me like I had my parents. Frank let me have my way with that and we didn't ever strike Hank. I still think we did the right thing, but when things go bad, it makes you rethink all the choices you made over a lifetime. I think it's natural.

Give us this day our daily bread...

Hank was about five when he started pinching on me. The first time he did it, I'd made him some oatmeal but forgot the maple syrup he liked so much. He just reached over and pinched me. Not just a small tweak, but a real twister. He took the skin in between his two little fingers, twisting hard while looking me in the face, and said *syrup*. I said, *we don't pinch* and *say you're sorry*, all the things a good mother is supposed to, but he just stared at me and repeated *syrup*. I got him the syrup.

And forgive us our trespasses…

I was embarrassed and didn't say nothing to Frank until he noticed the blue-yellow mark on my arm. He was fit to be tied. He yelled and carried on, threatening to blister Hank's behind, promise or no promise. But it'd happened days before and I didn't think little Hank would even understand what he was being punished for. He'd been such a good boy since that day. Truth be told, I was already feeling a bit afraid of upsetting him. I didn't know what would set him off. He never yelled or threw loud fits, just looked at me and waited until I saw things his way. If I held my ground, I might find a plant dumped over on the carpet or the pie I made for the church bazaar in the garbage can.

As we forgive those who trespass against us…

Hank got cleverer the older he got. There was the time that Frank had to say no about letting him go on a camping trip with the troop, we just didn't have the extra money, and Hank filled the gas tank with rocks. Frank had to bum rides or walk to work for weeks after that.

Hank never got into any real trouble at school. He had lots of friends and his teachers only had nice things to say about him. I think Frank was thinking the same as me, that over time Hank would calm down and grow out of it. But he just got more demanding. He kept on pinching me until I got enough sense to keep my arms out of the way. When he became a teenager, he started grabbing me above the elbow and pulling and squeezing until he got his way. He left so many bruises on me, I stopped noticing them. If Frank saw them, he never said a word. We'd stopped discussing Hank years before. There never seemed to be anything good worth talking about.

And lead us not into temptation…
Frank had a small heart attack after he retired. That's when Hank started with him. It was small things at first, like Frank reaching for a roll at dinner before Hank had his pick and getting his hand slapped back. We tried to laugh it off, but not long after that Hank started pushing Frank if he was in the way or moving too slow. Then I noticed the bruises on Frank's arms. That's when I knew I had to do something. Frank had worked his entire life to give that boy anything his heart desired and Hank owed his daddy more than to be using him as a punching bag. Frank deserved some respect and I was going to see he got it.

I thought about going to Reverend Wright, but he was new to the community and I didn't know him from Adam. I decided to talk to Hank's boss. I marched right into the police station, went straight to his office and said, *Captain Russell, my boy Hank has been hurting my Frank and it needs to stop.* Just like that. Then I went on to explain what Hank had been doing to his daddy. I didn't say nothing about what he'd done to me, since it'd stopped since Frank came home from the hospital. Captain Russell told me he would look into it and if he saw anything that needed to be done, he would take care of it himself. It'd been a burden for so long, I felt such relief after saying something. I didn't tell Frank. His pride would've been hurt and he would've been ashamed.

But deliver us from evil…
After I talked to the Captain is when Hank started bringing

the gun to the table. We had our dinner and I brought out dessert, blueberry crumble with vanilla ice cream, Hank's favorite, and he said, *Looks like somebody's been talking out of turn.* Then he put that gun next to his plate. *Captain Russell thinks family business should stay in the family. What do you think, Ma?* I nodded, because I knew that's what he wanted. Frank was really upset, but not me. Hank was never one to be challenged and I went and embarrassed him in front of his boss. I hadn't thought it all through at the time, but that gun helped me to see it clear.

Then Hank started talking up a blue streak about our age. He would say, *You two aren't getting any younger* and *I don't want to care for you the rest of my life.* We explained that we'd already taken care of all that. When the time came and one of us needed to go to a home, we would both go. Then he said that he didn't want to be shelling out his pay for us to be waited on hand and foot in one of those expensive old age homes. I explained that we had his daddy's pension and our Social Security to pay for all that. That's when he got angry and slammed his hand down on the table and told me to shut my yap. Poor Frank started shaking and I feared he would have another heart attack. I felt so bad for upsetting Frank. And for making Hank mad. It only makes things worse when he gets that worked up.

Hank had a different story every night after that, telling us what happens to old people when nobody wants them around anymore and the terrible things he saw people do to them. Frank and I just looked at our plates as Hank talked on and on.

For thine is the kingdom, the power and the glory…

Hank's stopped talking and is now doing. He's been real busy down in the basement. I saw him carrying a roll of clear plastic down the stairs the other day, then some buckets and sponges. I took a peek after he left for work. The windows had old blankets on them and the floor was covered with that plastic. Hank put two chairs facing each other in the middle of the room. I ran back up the stairs as fast as my old legs would take me and I threw up all my breakfast. I suppose it was fear. I've heard it does strange things.

Frank's started holding me real tight at night. We haven't been getting a wink of sleep. I think we're both afraid to close our eyes, for fear of what might happen when we open them back up.

For ever and ever...
Hank called in sick to work today. I know he's not sick because he ate a big breakfast of pancakes with maple syrup. I heard him tell Frank that he wants the two of us to come downstairs, that he has something to show us.

I'm not afraid. You decide when it's our time to go and have chosen our boy Hank to be your vehicle. I would've preferred You let nature take its course, but who am I to question your wisdom. I'm glad that Frank won't be left all alone without me. I worry about that sometimes. I should hurry. I don't want Frank going down them steps on his own. And I don't want to leave Hank waiting. It makes him angry. **Amen.**

A Slow Fall from a High Place

He stopped midpoint on the Brooklyn Bridge and took in the view of the city: the sun reflecting off steel, water butting against the shoreline, the towers, twin sentries, standing over it all. His family liked to tell the story about how his great-grandfather helped build the bridge. They say he lost his grip and fell to his death into the East River, leaving behind his wife and two children. His body was never recovered.

There were those in the family who insisted it wasn't true. They said he didn't die, that he walked away from his life. He left behind his responsibilities and disappeared into the city like a wisp of smoke. He became one of the stories told each year at Thanksgiving dinner as they passed the potatoes and oyster stuffing. His great-grandmother's brother had claimed to have spotted him eating lunch near the Jewish quarters a few years after he disappeared.

Even as a young boy, he knew what he was supposed to learn from the story: real men don't leave.

He chose to believe that his great-grandfather died so many years ago. He didn't want to have come from such weak stock, to think that his lineage included someone who would abandon those who depended on him. He wanted to believe the man made an error in judgment, that he had a slow fall from a high place.

*

It'd been almost four years since he and Tina, then six months pregnant, moved from their suburban house two miles from her parents in Pennsylvania. They were young, their future open before them, a baby boy on the way. With his salary, Tina could stay home after the baby came and decorate the two-bedroom brownstone that was over the bridge, close enough for him to walk to work.

When his father-in-law learned how much they paid for rent each month, he looked out at the view, swallowed hard as if he was trying not to get sick and said, "I hope you know what you're doing, son."

He smiled at the man and reassured him that yes, he definitely knew what he was doing.

Recalling his arrogance, his complete lack of humility, made him shudder.

Then he was fired. The words made him uncomfortable, like he was trying to write with somebody else's hand.

For three years, he'd worked long hours, rarely took a weekend off, never took a vacation. When Tina complained, he said it would pay off in the end. That she needed to be patient. That he was doing it for her and Gavin. He never said how much he loved it, felt that it gave him an identity, a purpose. He would leave work after the sun had gone down, crossing back over the bridge, certain he was leaving his mark.

Then Gavin got sick. They thought it was just a cold, but by the time they got him to the hospital, the doctors said it was pneumonia.

He called the office and told Mr. Hubert, his boss, that he was going to have to take a couple of personal days.

Silence on the line. He repeated himself.

"I heard you," Mr. Hubert said. "We all make choices in this life."

Fear rose up. He shoved it back down and went to sit with Tina next to Gavin's bed. He spent the next three days holding his wife's hand, stroking his boy's hair and worrying over Mr. Hubert's words. He knew the man was not what he appeared to be to others. That he spent most of his time keeping up the façade of a jovial entrepreneur, a compassionate boss, a man who cared about his clients. The first year at the job, he believed he was all of those things. It was Tina who pointed out that maybe what Mr. Hubert let the world see wasn't all there was to the man.

For the first company holiday party, Mr. Hubert took the senior staff and their spouses to a five-star restaurant in the city. Tina fretted for weeks about what to wear. He'd never seen his confident wife so nervous. Mr. Hubert bought bottle after bottle of the most expensive wine, spouting accolades to him and the others, raving about how much money they were clearing, making small, humorous jokes about how his wife liked spending his money at Barneys and how his kid's orthodontic work was keeping him from buying a Mercedes. By the time the main course arrived, Tina had grown quiet.

"You okay, hon?" he whispered in her ear as she picked at her sea bass.

She nodded and said, "Just a little tired is all."

In the cab on the way home, he sat back, enjoying his buzz and the way the lights of the city ticked past, the feel of Tina's hand in his.

"It was a beautiful restaurant," Tina said.

"Not as beautiful as you."

"Someone's feeling randy," she said.

"You betcha. Mr. Hubert liked you. I could tell."

"Hmm."

"What?"

She didn't reply, just looked out the window.

"What? He's great."

"I wouldn't say that."

His buzz started to diminish. "What're you talking about? He just dropped five g's on dinner for us."

"And spent the entire time belittling his family."

"He was just being funny."

"At their expense. His wife was mortified."

"She smiled the whole time."

"That was not a smile, it was a grimace."

"You're being ridiculous. That man's the reason we have this life."

Tina looked him full in the face and said softly, "You're the reason we have this life. I'm the reason we have this life."

"I don't want to argue."

"Just remember that anyone who talks badly about the people they claim to love will never treat you any different, okay?"

"Okay, Buddha."

When he went back to work, things changed. Mr. Hubert brought in another trader and they became thick as thieves, traveling together and taking three-hour lunches. He worked harder than before and tried to stay under the radar. After his two-year work-anniversary, Mr. Hubert started firing people. Within twelve months, four people were gone. He arrived at the office before Mr. Hubert and was in his chair when he left for the day. Only John Dolen had been with the company as long as him—everyone else was still wearing the glow of a new hire.

Then Dolen was let go. He helped carry his boxes to the waiting cab, trying to stay upbeat and encouraging.

"You're going to be okay. You're good at what you do. You'll find another position just like that." He tried to snap and almost dropped a box filled with office supplies that Dolen had pilfered from the supply closet.

"Thanks." Dolen tossed the box into the cab. "Be careful, man."

"I will," he said.

"You do know you're next, right?"

He shrugged and looked behind him to make sure no one from the office was within earshot.

"The guy's a nut," Dolen said as he got in the cab. "A real narcissist. I'd heard of them before, but never seen one up close."

He laughed uncomfortably at hearing Mr. Hubert talked about like he was an animal in the zoo.

"You can use me for a reference if you need to," he called out as Dolen closed the door. "Call me any time."

When he went back inside, Mr. Hubert stood behind the wall of glass that overlooked his employees. He smiled at him. Mr. Hubert didn't smile back.

He updated his resume and Tina started sending it out. Each morning, he crossed the bridge and went to work for a man he'd started to loathe. By the time Mr. Hubert got around to letting him go, he'd only had two interviews and neither had panned out.

The day he was fired, he didn't go home. He debated getting drunk at one of the bars near the office, but feared running into people he knew. He started walking and ended up at the museum. He and Tina had talked about going when they first came to the city. With Gavin being born just a few months after they arrived and his busy work schedule, there never seemed to be time.

He wandered around the exhibits, stopping at the Ming vases. *What is all this for?* he asked himself. *What is the purpose of all this if someday we'll just be gone?* He moved on to the jade combs. *We give ourselves tasks, little assignments we call jobs to keep us busy, then we die. Somebody once ran these combs through their hair. They felt the stiff bristles on their scalp. Now no one even knows who they were, remembers their name.* He studied the gold statues. He never worked for the money, but no one who knew him would believe that. He imagined they all saw him as a climber, not understanding that the money was just the cherry on top. Being a good worker, doing his job well, that was the reward. Without the work, who was he? He moved on to the paintings. *Artists get it*, he thought. *They know what it feels like to do something, create something for no reason other than the pure joy found in doing the work. A painter puts brush to canvas not knowing if anyone will ever want what he created, if money will ever be exchanged.* He studied Monet's haystacks. Painting after painting of the same thing. *That's me*, he thought, *I take pride in doing the same thing every day, just in a different light.*

The first two weeks after losing his job, he got up at the usual time, dressed in a suit, had a cup of coffee, kissed Tina and Gavin, and crossed the bridge. He had every intention of telling his wife that first day, when it was still raw, hurt so deep, but couldn't. He didn't want to have to act encouraging, be positive, make her feel better, feel safe. He wanted to walk the city he'd dreamed of living in since he was a boy.

The first week, he spent his days as a tourist. He went to the Statue of Liberty and took the tour, went to the platform of the Empire State Building and looked down on the world, had lunch in Central Park, spent an entire day at Times Square. The second week, he dived into the city, exploring the different pockets—Koreatown, Hell's Kitchen, Little Italy and Pakistan.

In the evenings, as he made his way back across the bridge with the taste of different foods from around the world still in his mouth, a heaviness settled in his chest and his muscles tightened. *I'll tell her tomorrow*, he promised himself each time he walked in the front door with his jaw clenched. Each morning he got up, pulled on his suit, and hurried back into the city. It was the first time in his life that he didn't have to be anywhere, wasn't on someone else's timetable, working toward someone else's deadline. He felt free.

Walking home on the Friday at the end of the second week, he knew it was time to come clean and tell Tina.

He stopped on the bridge and looked into the water below. He imagined falling into it from such a great height.

*

The next seven months were filled with forced optimism, consulting work pieced together from well-meaning friends, and job interviews that led nowhere. A few months in, Tina started taking Gavin to her parents for long weekends, leaving him alone to job search. He wondered if she knew he spent most of his time when she and Gavin were away going into the city, exploring bookstores and restaurants so hidden that only locals and daring tourists could find them.

Then the call from John Dolen came. He'd heard Mr. Hubert had fired him.

"I told my boss about you. He wants to meet on Tuesday morning. What do you think?" Dolen asked.

He hesitated, then remembered the pained look on Tina's face when they'd gone to the grocery store and had to use a calculator. He agreed to meet Dolen and his boss for a breakfast meeting at Windows on the World.

Someone bumped him as they hurried across the bridge. He checked his watch. The interview was in twenty minutes and he wanted to review his notes. He was going to get the job; he felt it in his bones. But he didn't want it and didn't know why. He imagined Dolen and his boss ordering coffee, reviewing his resume, discussing how much to offer and where they would negotiate.

He stayed on the bridge that might have been built by his great-grandfather and watched the boats go by.

Later, he'd recall hearing the plane before seeing it. At the time, it was just background noise, blending with the cars and the people passing behind him. When the plane hit, he thought it looked like a knife cutting through butter. People pushed past him, some screaming, others running. His feet stayed glued to the spot on the bridge. He watched as the second plane hit. As the towers, first one then the other, came down.

He started to call Tina. His hands shook and he almost dropped his phone. His body knew the horror even if his

mind did not. He started to dial. He stopped. He saw it all—
Tina hoping, praying he was alive. How she would wait all
night, calling her parents, his mother, keeping them updated.
How she would ask one of the neighbors to watch Gavin so
she could make her way closer to the destruction. The
pictures she would post around the city, not wanting to give
up hope. How, over time, she would grieve and move on.
He knew Tina would tell Gavin about him, how hard he
worked, how much he loved him.

He would become a better man than he ever truly was.

He held his phone over the railing and let go. As he
watched it fall, he said goodbye to the man he tried to be.

He crossed the bridge and walked into the city. Looking
back at the hole in the sky where the buildings had stood,
the plumes of smoke filling the air, he made a silent apology
to the great-grandfather he never knew for judging him so
harshly.

How Mai Ly Became a Cow

Once upon a time, not so many years ago, there was a young girl named Mai Ly who wanted nothing more than to be like her older cousin, Tin. Tin was only five years older than Mai Ly, but those years offered experiences that were thrilling to the younger cousin. When Tin moved to the city and found work, Mai Ly spent hours imagining what it would be like to be an independent woman living on her own. Then she received the letter from her cousin saying that the factory where she worked was hiring and Mai Ly could share her room. Mai Ly knew her real life was about to begin.

As the day grew closer for her to leave, the life Mai Ly lived with her grandmother and mother became lovely in its simplicity. Each night, her grandmother would brush Mai Ly's hair and tell the story of Cuoi, a young man who found a medicinal banyan tree that could bring back the dead.

"All he had to do was ensure that the banyan tree was safe. His selfish wife grew angry of the attention Cuoi showed the tree and, in her anger, tried to cut it down. To protect itself, the tree rose up out of the ground, roots and all. Cuoi grabbed onto its roots and he and the tree rose higher and higher into the sky. Now he lives on the moon with the banyan tree, caring for it and watching over all of us below."

"Me too?" Mai Ly would ask her grandmother.

"Especially you, my love."

Mai Ly felt safe knowing that Cuoi was watching over her, protecting her.

When Mai Ly arrived in the city, she gripped Tin's letter as she waited in the bus station, fearing her cousin had been changed so much by her new life that she would not recognize her. People arrived and departed, leaving only a handful of travelers sitting with their bags clutched tight.

"Are you waiting for someone?" an old mother sitting on the bench across from her asked.

Mai Ly nodded. "My cousin, Tin. She's meeting me here."

"Yes, Tin. She's a lovely girl."

"You know her?"

"We are good friends."

They laughed at the smallness of such a large world.

"Would you like a spring roll?"

Mai Ly took the treat, marveling at the kindness she was encountering in the city. She had heard many stories of mistreatment and deceit, those who wanted to take what was yours and make it their own. She reasoned that people always fear what they do not know, like Cuoi's wife and the banyan tree.

"Would you like me to take you to Tin? She lives near me. It is no bother."

Tin had been adamant in her letter that Mai Ly not leave the bus station without her, repeating it three times.

"Are you not waiting for someone?" Mai Ly asked.

How Mai Ly Became a Cow

"I'm just an old woman who likes to imagine a different life. You'll find one day that the soul still likes to travel even if the body cannot. I must leave now. Please let me take you to Tin. It is not safe for a young, beautiful girl alone in the city." Mai Ly blushed at the compliment. "If you were my daughter, I would want someone to do the same."

She scanned the room, hoping to see Tin, but feared that her cousin had forgotten her. As the old mother reached the door, Mai Ly called out, "Wait. I would be honored if you would take me to my cousin."

Mai Ly and the old mother drove through the city and into the countryside.

"Tin said she lived near the bus station," Mai Ly said.

"It is hard to get to by car. Things are different in the city."

Mai Ly watched the tall buildings grow smaller then disappear through the dirty car window. The old mother stopped in front of a small hut. There were no other buildings around.

"Is Tin inside?"

"She is waiting," the old mother said as she got out of the car.

Mai Ly followed her inside. There was a small wooden table with one chair and a pallet on the floor. No Tin.

"I forgot something in the car. Stay here," the old mother said as she dropped a bag on the table.

When she heard the car start, Mai Ly hurried from the hut. The taillights glowed bright in the darkness. She chased them until they disappeared.

Mai Ly paced the small space, afraid to stay and afraid to leave. She found a candle, matches and food inside the bag the old mother left on the table. Lighting the candle to chase the darkness from the small space, she spent hours spinning scenarios of why the old mother would leave her. She recalled half-whispered tales shared among the young girls in the village about those who had used poor judgment or been unlucky in circumstance. She berated herself for being foolish enough to go against Tin's instructions. For years, she had hung on her cousin's every word and when she had needed to heed her warning, all good sense had left her. Deciding she would walk back to the city at first light, she blew out the candle, lay down on the pallet and willed herself to sleep.

The sound of the door scraping on the dirt floor woke her. Confused, Mai Ly called out Tin's name, believing her cousin had found her. A middle-aged woman closed the door and spoke to her in a language she did not understand. When she saw that Mai Ly did not know what she was saying, she spoke in Mai Ly's tongue.

A large man with angry eyes stood behind the woman, blocking the door.

"Get up. It is time to go," the woman said.

"Did Tin send you?"

"You are to come with us."

"Are you taking me home?"

"You belong to me now."

Mai Ly stood and tried to run to the door. The large man grabbed her and threw her back to the pallet. The smile on his face showed how much he enjoyed it.

"If you do that again, I will leave you alone with Daiju. Believe me when I say that you do not want that to happen. Do you understand?"

Mai Ly nodded.

"Now come."

She followed the woman to a large truck. The back was covered with canvas. She was told to climb in. Two women were already inside, holding hands. She wanted to hold their hands, too, but did not know how to ask. She entwined her fingers, holding her own.

The truck filled throughout the day. By the time the sun had fallen, there were over twenty women in the back. The stories were all the same: An old mother approached them, spoke kind words, offered to find them work or take them to a family member, then they were taken to an out-of-the-way location and abandoned.

"Where are they taking us?" Li-Ying asked. She was fourteen with a heart-shaped face and large eyes. Daiju and the other guard had been staring at her since she was put in the truck. "What are they going to do with us?"

No one answered, only looked down.

When the truck stopped, the vibrations still moved through Mai Ly's body and sounded in her ears.

"Come cows. Move."

"Do not call us cows," Mei-Xie said. She had been one of the last women picked up. Anger smoldered in her eyes.

The woman smacked Mei-Xie's face. "I'll call you whatever I want."

Voices reached them through the darkness and they moved closer together. People surrounded them, pointing and laughing. The crowd parted as an old mother, Mother Ng, pushed through, her sons, Bohai and Chongan, close behind.

The woman and Mother Ng spoke, then they walked the line of captives, surveying them. Mai Ly kept her eyes on the ground.

Mai Ly and Li-Ying were taken from the line and told to stand away from the group. They clasped hands. Mother Ng spoke. The woman translated her instructions.

"Pull up your skirt," Mai Ly was told. She was too stunned to move. Mother Ng spoke again, this time slapping the ground at Mai Ly's feet. The woman translated, "Pull your skirt up and turn around."

Mai Ly looked to Li-Ying who had started to shake and cry. She turned and lifted her skirt. Mother Ng ran her gnarled hand down her back, then she slid her fingers inside Mai Ly, moving them in and out as if stuffing a duck. Mai Ly was too shamed to cry. Mother Ng then did the same to Li-Ying whose sobs moved through the dark night.

Mother Ng spoke to the woman and pointed to Mai Ly. "Bohai." Then at Li-Ying. "Chongan." Her sons smiled and slapped each other on the back.

The woman turned to Mai Ly and Li-Ying. "You two are to go with Mother Ng."

"Where?" Mai Ly whispered.

"You are the brides of the Ng brothers. Do not argue, this is an honor. Do not make Mother Ng think you are difficult."

Mai Ly and Li-Ying soon learned what it meant to be a Ng bride.

After the first night, Li-Ying went inside herself, found a safe place and decided to stay. She was sent to the tea plantation to work, no longer any good to her new groom. Mai Ly saw her from time to time. Her dark hair had streaks of white and her eyes no longer held life. Mai Ly didn't know if she should pity her or envy her.

Chongan pestered his mother endlessly, saying that Bohai had gotten the "good" bride. Mother Ng gave in and said that he could have Mai Ly, too, until the next round of girls came to the village. It was the first time Mai Ly spoke out. She received a beating from Bohai that was nothing compared to what she endured the first night she spent in Chongan's bed.

The year passed slowly for Mai Ly. She learned their language, but rarely spoke. Her days were spent working for Mother Ng and her two sons. At night, she would plead with Cuoi to leave his post on the moon and rescue her. As summer turned to fall, she found that she could no longer see her mother and grandmother's faces.

One day, Mother Ng followed her to the stream, carrying her bamboo stick and wielding it like an exclamation point.

"Go faster, Cow. We have much work to do today." Swish, swish, smack.

"Do not call me Cow. My name is Mai Ly. It is the name my mother gave me at birth." She had never spoken to Mother Ng in such a way.

"Your name is what I say it is." Swish, swish, smack.

Mai Ly dropped the buckets, the water splashing Mother Ng. She turned and walked away, ignoring Mother Ng calling after her.

"Come back, Cow. You must do as I say, you belong to me.

She made her way to the tea plantation that employed most of the people in the village. Walking the neat rows of tea trees, she thought of Cuoi on the moon, sitting under the Banyan tree. As the sun started to drop below the mountain, she returned home, convinced that Bohai would be easier on her in the dusky light of evening.

Bohai was sitting on the stool in front of the house, his stick, a twin to the one his mother used, across his lap. He pulled one last drag on his rolled cigarette, holding the smoke deep in his lungs as he ground the butt into the dirt.

When he raised the stick, Mai Ly did not flinch, knowing that her passivity irritated him. The beating would be worse, yet it was the only way she knew to hold tight to the girl she used to be. Bohai beat Mai Ly to the ground as the neighbors gathered to watch, gladness in their eyes. They believed the young woman needed to learn her place.

"Listen to Mother. She is your elder. You must respect her." He shook his head as he walked away, weary of teaching such a simple lesson to his willful wife.

She cleaned her cuts and bruises before making a supper of rice and fish. Afterwards, Bohai took her. With each thrust, she repeated "Mai Ly" so she would not forget.

The dream came to her that night. She was home. Her grandmother ran a jade comb through Mai Ly's hair, black ink flowing down her back. Her mother carried in banh chung, her favorite treat.

Mai Ly talked as if a cork had been removed, releasing all the words that had been denied for so long. She was lost in the joy of having people listen and failed to notice that her mother and grandmother were floating above her.

"What is happening, Mẹ? Ba ngoai?" she asked as they floated higher.

"You must go now, Mai Ly," her grandmother said.

"I want to stay."

"You must leave before it is too late," her mother told her. "Go now."

They dissolved. She was alone again.

How Mai Ly Became a Cow

She woke and listened to the sounds of Bohai sleeping deep and Mother Ng snoring in the corner of the room.

Slipping from the bed, she stepped over Mother Ng on her pallet and walked outside. The moon and Cuoi rested high in the sky. Mai Ly passed Bohai's stool and the square of dirt where she had cowered hours before. She glided past the neighbors' houses filled with those whose eyes had danced with each swing of the stick. Past Chongan's home, smaller and less impressive than his brother's, where he slept the sleep of an unsettled mind. She entered the rows of tea trees, her eyes fixed on the large mountain in the distance.

Mai Ly did not look back at the village until she crossed the small stream on the other side of the plantation. The mud sucked at her toes as if wanting to root her fast to the ground. She did not look long, fearing that she would conjure her sleeping jailers, alert them that she had gone.

As the moon balanced itself on the mountaintop, Mai Ly walked faster. Cuoi was still with her. She glanced back, but could no longer see the village. A weight lifted inside her chest. Her feet hurt. She did not care, as long as they kept moving her forward.

The grass blades no longer brushed her legs, but tickled her bare ankles. She was near a farm. Cows stood in a half circle, eating. One's teats were swollen and Mai Ly filled her hands with warm milk and drank until the empty ache in her belly eased. The cows moved closer, enclosing her in the center. She watched their yellow teeth grind the blades into mush. She looked into their dark eyes and wondered if the dark pools reflected a lack of thought or, like her, a deep knowing that they could not communicate. Mai Ly pulled her knees close to her chest and slept.

Running hooves woke her. Voices moved closer. Mai Ly tried to make herself small. She squeezed her eyes tight and prayed to Cuoi that they pass her by.

The swish, swish let her know that Mother Ng loomed above her.

Footsteps moved closer: Bohai and Chongan.

"Stand up, silly girl," Mother Ng demanded.

Mai Ly did not move.

"Why did you leave in the night? It is dangerous out here for you." Swish, swish.

"Why is she just laying there, Mother?" Chongan asked.

"Come, Mai Ly, we have much work to do," Mother Ng said.

Mai Ly opened her eyes and watched as the moon slipped behind the mountain. She knew then that Cuoi had never existed. No one was watching over her. No one was protecting her.

She uncoiled her legs, settling on her hands and knees. Filling a hand with grass, she shoved the moist blades into her mouth and started to chew. Around the growing mush, she said, "Do not call me Mai Ly. My name is Cow."

Safety Within the Silence

"This is the lady I was telling you about. Her son is the one who killed that boy. I think his name was Mitchell."

I stand outside the room and listen. I recognize the woman's voice. The day before, she'd been bustling around my 56-year-old cancer-riddled mother, cheerfully making small talk with me while adjusting the IV and rolling her patient from side-to-side, checking for bedsores.

"My aunt told me all about it. She worked on the boy when he was brought in. He was gone before they got him here."

"Can she hear you?" I don't recognize the voice of the other woman, but assume she's another nurse.

"Are you kidding me? She's so full of morphine she wouldn't hear a gun go off right in the room."

"You're terrible. You should be shot for that."

Both women laugh.

I know a good son, a better son, would rush into the room and shame the gossip-hungry women into an abrupt, uncomfortable silence. I wait. Years of being a topic of conversation has forced me to linger at doorways, listening to details of my life flow easily from the lips of strangers.

"What happened to the dead boy's family?"

"My aunt said they moved. This lady and her boy stayed in town but her husband left her after it happened. I can't believe they stayed. I wouldn't have."

"Me either."

"Have you seen the guy?"

"Is he the one who comes in the evenings?"

"That's him."

"He's so cute."

"You know what they say. The only ones still available are like toys at the bottom of the toy box—broken and no fun to play with."

I walk away, silently offering an apology to my mother for abandoning her to the thing she tried to protect me from for the past twenty years.

I imagine what I would say if I stepped into Room 216 and shared with the women the details of the worst day of my life. I would say: His name was Michael, not Mitchell. He was seven. His hair was curly blond and his eyes brown. He liked to ride his bike and eat orange popsicles.

I would tell them about how Old Lady Myers had been taken away by an ambulance a few days after summer vacation began. It was an exciting day for me with all the lights and activity. I didn't understand the gravity of what happened because my parents didn't tell me that the woman who'd given me butterscotch treats had died.

"A new family has moved into the Myers' place," is how I learned she wouldn't be coming back. "They have a boy your age. You should ask him if he wants to play."

I spent summer months playing alone or with visiting cousins. I'd never had a friend within walking distance.

I hurried to the backyard and watched his house. He came out his backdoor and we approached the chain-link fence that separated our yards, casting quick glances at each other. He was a little shorter than me. He said, *hey*. I said, *hey*. He smiled. I smiled. Our fates were sealed.

We played together every day and camped out in my backyard almost every night. It was during one of our overnights that he told me about the gun. It was his father's.

"I know where he keeps it. I'll show you if you want."

I don't want to see it, I lied. I let him convince me of my want and we agreed to search it out in the morning.

The next day, his mother stopped at the tent on her way to my house.

"Michael, don't forget you have to get a haircut later," were the last words his mother said to him.

We went in through the backdoor and into the kitchen. Michael opened a drawer and removed a key.

Why do you need that? I asked.

"It's locked up."

Even though we knew no one was home, we still tiptoed down the carpeted hallway. Our bare feet were covered with cut grass from the wet yard and we trailed it behind us on the way to his parents' bedroom. When we reached the door, he put his finger to his lips. His face was flushed and his nostrils flared from the excitement.

We went into the bedroom and opened the closet door.

"Lift me up, I can't reach."

I had trouble lifting him, but he was able to grab the shelf with one hand and pull down the gray metal box with the other. We sat on the closet floor, the light on above us, and stared at our find.

Open it, I whispered.

As he inserted the key and opened the box, I stood up and began hopping in place. He smiled, showing the gap from his missing teeth.

"Be careful," he said as he handed me the gun.

Its heaviness surprised me. It was cold. I held it with one hand and ran my fingers over and around the grooves. I wanted to feel every inch of it.

"You better give it back. I don't want to get caught."

I don't remember if I replied. I started to hand him the gun. I don't know if he was standing or still sitting on the closet floor. I remember the tug on the end of the barrel, but I don't remember pulling the trigger. I can still hear the shot and see the blood spreading like an angry blush across the front of his shirt.

I left my room the night it happened to get a drink of water and overheard my parents in the kitchen. My mother was crying and saying over and over, "It was an accident. He didn't mean to do it."

"Ignorance isn't an excuse, not even from a child," was the only thing I heard my father say about it as I stood in the shadows. He left soon after, went to Alaska to work on the pipeline. At first, the letters he sent home said he would be back soon. We both knew different. He got as far away from the talk of the town as he could without falling off the continent. It was too hard for him to look at his thoughtless son, so he chose not to look at me at all. The last time we spoke was when he called to say he wouldn't be coming home for my high school graduation. I told him it was okay. I told him I understood.

My mother and I only talked about it once. In Room 216, after she was admitted to the hospital for what we both knew would be the last time. I was hanging around, paying regular visits to the soda and candy machines, feeling useless. She was floating on a cloud of painkillers and feeling talkative.

"Can you believe your cousin Vera is getting married for the third time in seven years?" she said as I flipped through a magazine. I looked up when I realized she'd stopped talking and was staring at me.

"Do you remember that day?" she whispered.

I didn't have to ask her what day.

Yeah, I remember, I said. Heat flooded my face and neck.

"I should've asked you a long time ago. I didn't want to remind you, in case you'd forgotten."

I nodded.

"How do you tell a seven-year-old that it wasn't his fault when it was, even if he didn't mean to do it? I didn't want to lie to you, so I didn't say anything." She started to cry.

It's okay, Mom. I'm okay, I said, trying to soothe her.

She kept saying, "poor boy" over and over. I wasn't sure if she meant me or Michael.

I wish I'd told her that I understood how difficult it must've been for her, sitting in her kitchen on that bright, summer morning sipping coffee with her new friend, a friend she'd desperately wanted. They would've been talking about their plans for the day when they heard the shot. How, with a mother's instinct, they both would've gone still. I wanted to tell her that it was okay to have hoped that it wasn't her son—it wasn't selfish, only human.

I wanted to let her know that I couldn't imagine the loneliness she must've felt after my dad went away. The emptiness in their bed was a nightly reminder of the damage

I'd caused. Or how each time I was overlooked for a birthday party or stood watching the other kids play, the tightening of her jaw and the fierce grip on my hand let me know that the sound of that shot made us partners in my crime.

I wanted to tell her all these things. I didn't. Her memories are hers and I have no right to intrude upon them. She taught me well. There is safety within the silence.

Of all these things, I wish I'd shared with her Michael's last minutes. I never tried to reach out, let him know he wasn't alone. I took his life, but I wasn't equipped to witness it seeping away.

At night, while waiting for sleep to come, I see him holding his hands over the spreading red and hear the words he cooed to himself like a mother trying to soothe her frightened child, "It's okay, Michael. You're going to be okay."

His words follow me into sleep where he waits for me to chase him through the night. Michael lives on, always a step ahead of me. I know I'll never outrun him.

Denial Can Be a Beautiful Thing

If anyone asks me about Martin, my husband of forty-two years, three months, and eight days, I always say the same thing, He was a good man, bless his soul. The day the heart attack took him was the hardest day of my life.

The women tsk-tsk, rub my back and age-spotted hands, and the men nod knowingly. Most of them have been there, on the other side of a couple, left alone to navigate their final years in a strange place, forced to make new friends, eat meals served on someone else's schedule from someone else's menu.

What I never say, never bring into the light to be examined, scrutinized, judged, is how the man I married the year I turned twenty picked me, an unripe peach, and left me to rot.

When I met Martin, I was drawn to his vitality and the ease he had in his own skin. His laughter would ring through a crowd and pull people to him like homing pigeons. If I'd been more worldly, I would've noticed that those who surrounded him were men—men who snickered behind their hands whenever I came near.

During my more generous moods, I console myself with the knowing that it was a different time, people weren't as open-minded as they seem today. They were quick to judge the unknown, trapped in hand-me down beliefs they gripped tight like car keys and wallets. I try to imagine what it was like for Martin, trapped inside a knowing of who he was but unable to live within it. He needed a certain kind of life and had to settle for… That's where I stop, knowing that *I* was what he settled for. My level of self-honesty can only be taken so far if I have any hope of staying intact.

When my thoughts become smoky black, I ask, *Why me*? What about me made Martin think that my life would be so less than ordinary that there would be no loss if he wasted my years in a loveless marriage full of lies and deceit? What had he seen that first night at my parents' country club, the one they'd pinched and saved for in order to join, trying to fit in, pretending they were more than they were? Did he spot me from across the room in my handmade gown, the one I'd spent hour upon hour stitching, imagining myself transformed into a glamorous princess in gold taffeta, and discern all my insecurities, all my uncertainties, and decide that I would be the perfect dupe to wash his clothes, cook his meals, scrub his toilets? My deepest fear is that the answer is yes—that was exactly what Martin had thought.

The one and only time I tried to share my fears was almost a year to the day after our June wedding, an absurd anniversary that sat like dead weight on my chest. It was so long ago. When I close my eyes, I can see me and my dear sweet Dorie, my closest friend since grade school, my touchstone and confidant, in all our youthful beauty, sipping iced tea on the veranda, the sun starting to slip low in the sky. We did everything together—school dances, sleepovers, long hours of talking about the men we would marry and how many babies we would each have: two for

Dorie, twin boys, and five for me, I liked the way "a handful" felt in my mouth. Martin peeked his head out the sliding glass door and told me not to wait up, he was going out with the boys.

"I was going to make that meatloaf you like," I told him, the eagerness in my voice making me blush.

"Save me some, I'll eat it later. Bye, chickies."

I stared into my glass and listened as Martin's car backed out of the drive and headed away from me and the home I'd tried to make.

"He sure is handsome," Dorie said.

I forced a smile. "Our wedding photos look like something from *Picture Play*."

Martin had looked dashing in a white tuxedo with black tie and cummerbund and I'd worn an A-line Dior, my hair in a French pleat with a birdcage veil covering my eyes, making everyone and everything fractured and gauzy.

"Do you ever worry? With him going out so much and all?"

"A little. Do you worry about Saul?" Dorie had gotten married a few months before to her high school sweetheart.

"Not for a second. That man knows what's best for him."

We laughed, knowing what Dorie said was true. Saul was a meek man with a heart that beat only for her. My laughter turned into tears.

"Are you okay?" Dorie asked, taking the glass from my hand and replacing it with a napkin.

"I don't know what's wrong with me," I lied.

"Are you preggers? I heard that does crazy things to your emotions."

I cried harder.

"There, there. It can't be that bad, can it?"

The words tumbled out. "I don't think he loves me."

"Of course he does. He married you."

"I don't know why. He's never here and when he is, he barely speaks to me."

"That's just the way some men are."

"Is that the way Saul is?"

"No, but he doesn't count."

I hesitated before adding, "And he sleeps in the guest room."

"Why?"

"I think I disgust him."

"That's not possible, Nora. You're beautiful. It must be something else. Do you snore?"

"How would I know?"

"How was the honeymoon?"

"Hawaii was lovely. I showed you the photos."

"I mean, how was the *honeymoon*?"

I looked at my dear friend, someone I'd never lied to and trusted with all my wants and fears, and thought about Martin's insistence that we get two hotel rooms, claiming that he had trouble sleeping at night and didn't want to keep me awake. I left girlhood behind that day when I chose not to burden Dorie, a person I loved, with something she couldn't control.

"It was fine."

"Just fine?"

"It was good. I'm just being silly. Who knows, maybe I am pregnant."

Dorie didn't look convinced, but didn't push the issue.

Over time, I accepted my situation, even though I wasn't quite clear yet what the situation was. That would demand late night drives where I followed Martin to out-of-the-way bars as well as countless phone calls from strange men demanding to speak with my husband without even a polite hello. Five years into our marriage, Martin shared his predilection, followed by a promise to stay if I never mentioned a word of it to anyone—including him. I agreed and settled in, choosing to live in the ugly embrace of denial.

In my confusion and loneliness, I threw myself into volunteer work where I learned that I had a knack for numbers and for getting people to do things for free. During those early years, I wanted nothing more than to step inside the closed box that was my husband's life, be invited in and settle with him, know him as any wife would. The invitation never came. He had his life and I had mine. Then we started *Around the World Travel Agency*. It became the largest agency in the city. Those years were the best of my life. During the day, I had Martin all to myself, only having to give him up when we locked the doors and he rushed off to parts better left unknown.

Martin died on a cruise in the Mediterranean, leaving almost everything to me. The only stipulation he made in his will was for a hundred-thousand dollars to go to a man named Roger. I told the lawyer to send it, along with a box of Martin's shirts, all of his jewelry except his wedding band, and an old picture I'd found of him taken on one of the Greek islands. His face was a rich walnut brown and he wore a contented look I'd never been witness to. My husband claimed that his travels to Greece were to re-energize and reconnect with himself. I realized that Martin's trips were a way to get away from me and to be with someone else.

I was stunned that after all the years of being lied to and discarded, I could still feel betrayed by one of Martin's half-truths.

I returned to the travel agency after the funeral, but my husband had taken the excitement of running it with him to the grave. I sold it to two agents who'd been with us for years, boxed up the house, put everything in storage, and went to Greece.

I went from one island to the next. First Corfu, where I spent my days walking from one end of the island to the other, looking into the faces of strangers, running my hands over the stucco walls as if trying to conjure a version of the truth that would help me rest easy and find peace. I moved on to Crete followed by Rhodes, and ended on Mykonos— all the time searching for something I wouldn't find.

On Mykonos, I heard a man's laughter floating from across the bar. Hurrying over, I expected to find Martin, forgetting that I'd seen him laid out in the coffin with the pearl satin liner. Instead, I found a group of four young people—two men, two women—confident in their youth and beauty, enjoying the sun, drink and company. They grew still when they saw me staring; growing uneasy in the quiet, they moved away. I chased after them, trying to make them understand how silence could feel like a slap and a turned back could bruise a soul, leave it tender to the touch.

That was my bleakest moment. I considered going to Milos and throwing myself headfirst into the island's volcano, my gray hair unbound, tendrils of lost years trailing behind me. Instead, I returned to the hotel and milked a sunburn that settled in my wrinkles and stung when I tried to cover the painful red with face powder.

The sunrises were what I took away from the trip. Each morning, I slipped from between the rough hotel sheets, pulled on my robe, made myself a cup of coffee, and sat on the balcony to watch the sun come up. I'd rarely considered God, feeling that if there was one, He never would have made Martin into the man he was. Those mornings, sitting alone, sipping my strong, sweet coffee and witnessing the slow peek of the bright sun, I felt connected to life, as if there was a reason for everything and the answers were hidden in the crystals of color reflected all around me.

After returning to the States, I had my things removed from storage, put into a moving truck, and taken south. Dorie and Saul had moved to Florida when their first granddaughter was born ten years before and had been urging me to join them at the Mayflower Retirement Community, a name that conjures women in petticoats and caps, men in black waistcoats and silk stockings. I don't know if the name is a sardonic play on words referring to the unavoidable journey we residents are about to embark upon or the new, unfamiliar setting we find ourselves in, geriatric pilgrims on our last adventure.

Houses we worked a lifetime cleaning, spackling, lawns meticulously mowed were replaced with emergency on-call buttons and two bedroom bungalows ill-equipped to contain a lifetime of furniture, memories and disappointments. The first time I went to the dining hall for dinner and saw a sea of white hair and gleaming pates, the phrase "God's waiting room" sprang to mind. It sent a quick chill down my spine. With a deep breath, I pushed my shoulders back as far as I could—years of carrying Martin's lie had rounded my shoulders and slightly bowed my back—and followed Dorie and Saul to their table.

Then I met Cory. His t-shirt caught my eye. It was a picture of Santa Claus, his pants pulled down, with a bullseye on his behind. Rudolph stood behind him holding a shotgun. He saw me looking and laughed.

"I don't get it either. My grandson bought it for me."

"Is it revenge? Did Santa try to shoot Rudolph at some point? Was he craving venison stew?" I asked, absent-mindedly searching through my mail.

"You think its self-defense? Santa went mad, the holiday stress and all, and went on a rampage. Every reindeer for himself. Go Donner! Go Blitzen! Run away! Run away!"

"I think the better question is why your grandson holds such hatred for Saint Nick?"

"Maybe it's because he's Jewish."

We laughed and he held out his hand. "I'm Corrigan, but call me Cory, everyone does."

We started spending time together. At first, it was inviting him to sit with me and my friends during meals. Before long, we became one of those morphed couples where everyone referred to us as one entity: NoraandCory— CoryandNora. It was assumed that if one of us was attending the string concert in the park or the luau in the courtyard, the other would be there. I didn't know how to react. Although I'd been married, a couple of sorts, I'd been a lone attendee in my social life. Martin and I seldom went out together and when we did, when there was no way for him to excuse his absence, usually funerals and weddings, he would scan the room for someone more interesting and leave me to fend for myself in the crowd.

The first time Cory kissed me, two months after our initial meeting, I turned my cheek to him out of habit. Martin wasn't a man to show me affection and a quick peck was all he allotted, doled out on holidays and birthdays. An apology was given by Cory as he hurried across the trimmed lawn to his bungalow. I didn't know the protocol for such a situation. Should I follow him and try to explain? Wait for him to seek me out? I debated calling Dorie, but felt foolish for not knowing how to handle the situation at my age. I did nothing. A familiar act that was like an old friend.

Cory stayed to himself, or at least away from me, for the next week. It was painful, knowing that his absence by my side was noticed by those who inhabited our small world. As I'd done in the past, when things became unbearable, I planned a trip. The imagined locale and the productive search had always calmed me. I decided to go somewhere exotic and settled on Sri Lanka. I envisioned hiking through the tropical forests I'd heard about from my more daring clients, a beautiful flower tucked behind one ear, monkeys chattering in the trees. How I would navigate such an escapade with my bad knees was a detail I chose to ignore.

Two days before I was to leave there was a tentative knock at my door. It was Cory. He wore a t-shirt with "Retired: Don't Ask Me To Do a Damn Thing" across the front.

"I like your t-shirt," I said, unable to think of anything clever to offer. "Grandson?"

"I just don't have the heart not to wear them. It's a strange obligation I never thought I'd feel."

I invited him inside and busied myself by making coffee.

"I want to apologize to you," Cory said after I handed him a cup—two sugars, no cream—and settled at the table across from him. "I made a mess of things. It's been a long time."

I didn't have to ask him a long time for what. The courting rituals my peers and I performed were as distant as high school dances and black-and-white televisions.

"No, you didn't. I did."

"Please don't think that. I should never have presumed that you were interested in an advance from me."

"But I was." I blushed. "I am."

"Then why did you turn away?"

"Fear, I suppose. Or habit." I wanted to add more. Wanted to tell him about the years of craving the touch of a man who chose to make his shame my own. That over time, I convinced myself that I was not good enough for Martin to love. Wanted to tell him how it was easier to let those who cared for me believe I was barren than share that I'd never lain with a man, stepped into the world where grown women reside.

Cory stood, reached for my hand and pulled me to my feet. He kissed me, running his hands up my back. It was a luxurious feeling, one I'd never experienced. He kissed my neck and my knees went weak.

"I need to tell you something," I whispered into Cory's right ear. I knew he couldn't hear out of it which was the reason for his keeping me on his left whenever we went out together. "I've never had relations with a man."

When he didn't stop kissing me, I gifted myself with one last lie: He heard and doesn't care.

As I stepped into a new life, a second chance, a do-over worthy of being printed on one of those t-shirts Cory's grandson finds such joy in, I decided that denial can be a beautiful thing.

A Promise Made

"He's about to die, don't ya know," Timothy heard Mrs. O'Malley say to the other women pinning their underthings and sheets to the clothes line. "He's got the consumption. He just got that new leg this past year and now it'll go to waste, just sit in a cabinet until it's thrown out with the rubbish. What a shame." The women agreed that it truly was a shame.

He tried to look as if he wasn't listening. Mrs. O'Malley caught him. "What're you doing there, Timothy Doyle? Don't you have nothin' better to do than stand around listenin' to old ladies talk amongst themselves? Get home with ya, before I cut a switch."

His face burned as he tucked his crutch under his right arm and turned for home.

"And tack up your pant leg. It's draggin' behind ya like a bad thought," Mrs. O'Malley called after him.

Timothy ignored her and kept walking. It was his secret that the weight of the material dragging heavy below his right knee where the rest of his leg should've been made him feel whole. Mrs. O'Malley and the other women could never understand—there was no part of them that was missing.

Timothy passed the boys playing football and, for the first time, imagined joining them. He would run fast and kick hard, his crutch a bad memory. Maybe I'll throw it on the fire, he thought, picturing his crutch engulfed in flames. It made him smile.

The thought of benefitting from Mr. Flannigan's misfortune made him feel ashamed. Mr. Flannigan was always nice to Timothy, going out of his way to give him a piece of candy when his ma took him into the Flannigan's grocery store. The extra attention embarrassed him, made him feel flawed, even though he knew it was meant to make him feel special.

The first time he saw Mr. Flannigan without his crutch, standing straight, moving with a limp and a confidence that was new, he asked his ma, "Did it grow back?"

"Don't be daft, Timothy," she told him. "Body parts that are missing don't grow back. He bought it."

"Can I get one?"

The closed look on her face let him know that the answer was no.

I'm not happy he has the consumption, he reassured himself as he made his way home. *I wouldn't wish consumption on Mr. Flannigan, or anyone for that matter, but since he already has it, it's not as if I cursed him, not at all. But when he dies, it would be a shame, as Mrs. O'Malley said, to let that leg of his go to waste.*

The next morning, he told his ma he was going to the Church. Margaret Doyle never made her children explain why they needed to go to St. Ignatius, believing that it was a private thing between Father O'Connor, the sinner and God.

Timothy knew he was going to have to confess the lie in the confessional. He didn't care. It was the first time

A Promise Made

Timothy had felt such an intense need that he was willing to commit all the sins in the Bible to get what he wanted. The leg was owed to him. Sooner or later God had to make right what was done wrong.

By the time he made it to the Flannigan's store, his shirt was stuck to his chest, showing his ribs through the thin material.

The store's front doors were locked and Timothy couldn't see anyone inside. He sat down on the steps and tried to calm himself. Disappointment pressed on his chest, making breathing hard. He hadn't considered that Mr. Flannigan might die before he could ask him for his leg. Now he feared he was too late.

"Timothy Doyle, what're you doing sitting there on the steps like that?" Mrs. Flannigan asked as she unlocked the door. "You look like a poor urchin. Your ma would be appalled."

"I was just resting."

"Does your ma need something from the store?" She went back inside and Timothy followed her as she bustled about putting things on the counter.

"No, Ma'am. I came to see how Mr. Flannigan is doing. I heard he was ill and I wanted to see if he was better," he told her, staring at the ground. He knew his face was red and he hoped she didn't notice.

In the silence, he looked at her. There were dark circles under her eyes and a small, sad smile on her lips.

"He's very sick, Timothy."

"Is it the consumption?"

She said no, that it was something he'd been sick with for a time.

"Can I see him?"

She hesitated before saying, "I suppose. Only for a bit. He tires quickly. Does your ma know where you are?"

His first instinct was to lie and say yes, but she was being so kind, he couldn't.

"No, Ma'am."

He prepared himself for the lecture of what a bad boy he was, but she only said, "It'll be our secret. No more lying."

"Yes, Ma'am."

"Go up those stairs. It's the second door on the right. If he's sleeping, don't wake him. His sleep is troubled. The doctor gave him something this morning," she told him. "He might not know who you are at first. Give him time, it'll come to him."

At the top of the stairs, an odor like the back entrance of the butcher shop filled the hallway. When he opened the door to Mr. Flannigan's room, he had to swallow hard to keep from gagging. This is what dying smells like, he thought.

A small amount of light filtered through the curtains. He waited for his eyes to adjust before moving closer to the bed. Timothy thought Mr. Flannigan was asleep, then he turned his head toward the table that held pill bottles and a pitcher of water.

"Pour me some water," he said.

Timothy filled the glass and held it out to Mr. Flannigan until he realized the man was too weak to hold it himself. He put the glass to his lips so he could drink a small amount before falling back onto the pillow.

Timothy's eyes were used to the dim room and he spotted the leg propped in the corner near the bed.

"Mr. Flannigan, do you remember me?" His voice shook and he cleared his throat. "I'm Timothy. Margaret Doyle's boy."

"I know who ya are." Timothy was encouraged by Mr. Flannigan's voice. It still sounded like him, only very tired.

"Sir, I was wondering if I could ask you for something?"

"What do ya need?"

"First, I want to say how sorry I am that you're sick." Timothy was unsure of how to continue. He'd practiced his speech all the way to the store, now he didn't know if there was a polite way to ask a dying man for his leg. "Second, I was just wondering, if you're not going to get better, which I hope you do, but if you don't, could I have your leg? You won't be needing it anymore because my ma always tells me that in Heaven those who are not whole, they become whole. So you'll be getting a new leg when you get there and Mrs. Flannigan will just throw your old one out." He cleared his throat again. "Maybe I could take it? I don't have any quid, but if I had your leg, I could make some and give it to your wife and she could have some extra."

Timothy tried not to stare at the leg as he waited for Mr. Flannigan's answer.

Mr. Flannigan started to laugh and motioned Timothy closer. "You can have the damn thing. You're right, I won't be needing it anymore. Just take it after I'm in the ground, boy." He was still chuckling to himself as he slipped back into sleep.

Leaving the room, Timothy stopped at the leg. He wanted to take it in his hands, try it on, see what it felt like to stand straight, to be complete. He resisted, knowing that he would have plenty of time with it and right now, it was still Mr. Flannigan's leg.

He thanked Mrs. Flannigan on his way out the door. On the way home, he said hello to everyone he saw, even Mrs. O'Malley who demanded to know what he thought he had to be happy about. He didn't bother to answer, knowing she would never understand.

He stopped at St. Ignatius, went up the stairs, genuflected and left. He didn't want to have lied to his ma and now he hadn't. Not really.

"What're you grinning at Timothy Doyle?" his mother asked him as she got up to clean the dishes. "You look like the cat that got the mouse."

"I'm happy."

He didn't want to tell her about his good fortune, he wanted to show her. She'd never seen him complete and he imagined walking in the door, carrying a bundle of wood for the stove instead of a handful of sticks. He knew she would cry, but they would be tears of joy.

"Happiness looks good on you, sweet boy," she told him.

He spent the next few days in a blissful fog, lost in a world that did not yet exist. Timothy no longer listened with envy to the other children playing, but watched them, so he would be prepared to join in. He no longer worried himself about the stairs at school, knowing they were no more than a temporary inconvenience. Even his school work had become something to be done and put aside, no longer checked over and over in the hopes of a word of praise from the teachers.

A few days after his visit to the Flannigans, as his family sat down for supper, the church bells sounded.

"Mr. Flannigan passed away this noon," his ma told them. "His poor wife, she's all alone now, never having any children. It's a shame."

Timothy pictured the Flannigans the day he'd gone to the store. Mrs. Flannigan, tired and sad; Mr. Flannigan in the dim light, coated in the smell of death. Then he imagined the leg waiting for him in the corner of Mr. Flannigan's bedroom.

His ma said the wake was in the morning and the funeral was at noon time.

"Can I go?" Timothy asked.

"Why would you want to be going to Mr. Flannigan's funeral? We are in no way family to those people."

"I want to pay my respects," he told her as he stared at his plate.

"That's kind and all, but I think we should just take some bread to the family. We don't need to be intruding on their sorrow."

Timothy lay awake that night trying to figure out how he was going to get to the funeral so he could get his new leg. He wondered if Mr. Flannigan would be wearing it at the wake. He wasn't sure how he felt about having a leg that had been on a dead man. He quickly put the thought from his mind. His ma had said enough times that beggars could not be choosers and Timothy was a smart enough lad to understand that if you had to ask a dying man for his leg, you were a beggar.

When his ma woke him for school, Timothy said he wasn't feeling well.

"You'll have to care for yourself today. I can't miss work," she told him, tucking the blankets tight around him.

After the others left, he got out of bed, put on his Sunday best and left for the funeral. The rubbish-filled alleys were difficult to maneuver, worse than the muddy roads, but Timothy had to stay off the roads so no one would see him. Twice, he tripped over empty bottles, cutting his chin and scratching his palms.

It took him longer than he planned to get to the grave site. As Timothy moved closer to the small group of mourners, he heard Father O'Connor praying for Mr. Flannigan, "O God, by whose mercy the souls of the faithful find rest; mercifully grant forgiveness of their sins to Thy servants and handmaids, and to all here and elsewhere who rest in Christ: that being freed from all sins, they may rejoice with Thee forevermore."

Father O'Connor went on to talk about what a devout Catholic Mr. Flannigan had been. Timothy tried not to smile. Mr. Flannigan had snored through most services, not even standing when it was time for Communion.

He then told the mourners of the farm accident that Mr. Flannigan had been in when he was a boy that caused him to lose his leg. Timothy had always imagined that it had been something more exciting. He didn't judge. It was still more interesting than just being born that way.

"It gives me such joy to release Joseph Flannigan to the Lord as a complete man. I've been told that Joseph saved every extra quid he made for many a year to be able to purchase his artificial leg. His wife told me that he was so proud to have both feet on the ground once again that he never wanted for another thing. We put Joseph Flannigan into the hands of the Lord with both feet on the ground."

Timothy pushed his way to the front of the crowd. Gasps and angry mutterings followed him. He didn't care.

"Mrs. Flannigan, please, I must talk to you," he said as he reached the new widow. She'd been crying, but stopped because of the commotion. "Did Mr. Flannigan say anything to you about his leg?"

"You're bleeding, Timothy. What happened?" she asked.

"Did he say anything about me?"

"Move along, Timothy," Father O'Connor said.

"Leave me be. I need to know if he told her."

"You're disrespecting the dead, young man," Father O'Connor said. He took Timothy's arm and tried to move him away from Mrs. Flannigan.

Timothy twisted away and swung his crutch at the priest's legs. The mourners gasped. Two men grabbed Timothy by the arms and carried him out of the cemetery. His cries from outside the cemetery walls were carried to the mourners as Mr. Flannigan's coffin was covered in dark earth, holding Timothy's birthright, the wholeness that was his due.

Never Above the Tiara

For Eric Still

During summer vacations, my mom made me go with her to Ruby's Salon. Each Tuesday, I would flip through magazines that told women how to make easy summer desserts and when to wear white. I couldn't seem to retain the information, so each time I read the articles, they were new and, the year I turned fifteen, disdainful.

"My friends are out having fun and I'm stuck listening to a bunch of old women talk about nothing," I said when we stopped at the only stoplight in town. A feeling of restlessness had settled in my limbs. It was a new feeling and not knowing what it was made me jittery and mean.

"You're off with your friends every day. I call dibs on Tuesdays."

"Call dibs," I repeated, the sarcasm dripping from my tongue.

My mom's hands tightened on the wheel until her knuckles were white. It made me feel powerful and a little afraid. The Friday before, I'd spent the night at my friend Josy's house, eating junk food and watching horror movies. Josy made a joke about her mother's cooking and Mrs. Harlen smacked her in the mouth. You won't disrespect me,

Mrs. Harlen said as she walked out of the room. It was the first time I'd seen a grown woman hit anyone and I couldn't shake the feeling that everyone, even my mom, had their limits.

"I'll get my hair done and then we'll have lunch. After that, you can go to the pool with Josy. Okay?"

"I guess so," I mumbled to the passenger side window.

"Start thinking about where you want to eat."

I didn't respond. I hadn't planned on going to the pool, but didn't want her to know. I was having cramps and didn't want to risk starting my period in the water. I'd started over winter break, later than all of my friends, and the excitement quickly changed to fear when I saw the blood spotting my underwear. The idea that it would happen every month for most of my life seemed cruel and possibly unhealthy.

Ruby's was on the corner of Main and Chestnut, across the street from the Depot Restaurant and the Iron Horse Tavern. I knew we'd have lunch at the Depot and would laugh when the train passed, shaking our glasses and rattling the silverware. What I really wanted was to go inside the Iron Horse, see what it was like. I'd walked past once and saw, before the large door closed, people perched on bar stools, cigarette smoke like halos around their heads. Some sat hunched over drinks, others rested their backs on the bar, talking to friends or listening to the music pouring from the juke box. I tried to tell Josy what I'd seen. She shrugged and told me her uncle used to go there before he joined the Army. "My grandma said he smelled like a heathen after being in there."

I didn't know what a heathen was, but, at fifteen, I was sure I wanted to smell like one.

By the time we walked from the car to Ruby's, beads of sweat coated my hairline and my t-shirt was stuck to my back. It'd been the hottest summer in years, at least that's what my dad kept repeating to anyone who would listen.

Ruby had fashioned the salon after her name—the walls were a deep red and the chairs were a lighter red, not quite pink. The floor was made up of white and red squares. A large ruby gem stone was proudly displayed on the wall above the dryers. Ruby's dream was to get one that lit up.

Ruby was finishing up with Mrs. Brubaker and Mrs. Collingsworth was already under the dryer when we went inside, the cold air conditioning hitting us hard, making us sigh. I'd known both women since birth. And I knew that Mrs. Brubaker's husband was fighting cancer and Mrs. Collingsworth had a large bunion removed from her big toe that spring. I'd learned all of that the week before. When I got home, I searched through the B encyclopedia so I could see what a bunion looked like. At the pool, I studied all the feet around me, searching for them, a strange eye-spy game I played by myself.

When I was younger, the women would fawn over me, asking me about my summer and what I wanted to be when I grew up. That summer they mostly ignored me, only acknowledging me with darting glances when they talked about something they thought might not be appropriate for me to hear.

Clara Peterson came into the shop as Ruby was finishing up my mom's hair. She was a few years older than me and we'd ridden the same bus. I knew her but she didn't know me. My friends and I would watch her as she walked down the school bus aisle, her long hair swinging side to side. We would twist in our seats, acting like we were talking to each other, but really watching Clara with the other seniors. Every once in a while, she would lean forward and pull her honey-colored hair over one shoulder, then lean back. My friends started pulling theirs to the side, no matter the length. I wanted to tell them that Clara was doing it because her rug of hair would catch between her back and the bus seat, not as a flirtation or out of vanity, but I knew it wouldn't have mattered. We all knew, without having to be told, that Clara had "It." She was born to drag eyes to her. It wasn't something she asked for, it'd been gifted upon her the way others were gifted with the ability to sing or draw. Clara was meant to be seen.

No one was surprised when Paul Steeger started driving her to school senior year. If anything, most people wondered why it hadn't happened sooner, why it had taken the two so long to come together. They were like two planets that had been in the same orbit, on opposite sides of the sun.

Clara waited by the door until my mom slipped from Ruby's chair, then she hurried to it. We could all see that she was sitting on some of my mom's cut hair, pieces clinging to her shoes.

While she waited, she stared at her reflection, not blinking. Ruby fastened the smock around her neck. The only sounds were the woosh-woosh from the hair dryers and the brush moving down the length of her thick hair. The dark blue and purple bruise that bloomed around her left eye and down her cheek looked like a child's first attempt with watercolors. I thought the colors lovely against Clara's light skin.

Ruby stopped brushing and asked her what she wanted done. Clara's lips moved, but no one, including Ruby, could hear her. Leaning closer, Ruby asked her to repeat herself.

Ruby lifted the weight of Clara's hair and put it in a low hanging pony tail. She hesitated, then asked, "Are you sure, dear?"

A slight dip of her chin let everyone know that yes, she was sure.

Clara had been voted prom queen two years running. Her senior year, she rode the bus the Monday after prom, the first time in months, giving the mundane trip an electric charge. The tiara was perched on top of her head, but facing the wrong way. The younger kids at the front of the bus giggled as she passed. My friends and I only cast quick glances at each other and shrugged.

"Hey Clara, you know you're wearing that thing backwards?" Sam Docket asked so that the entire bus could hear.

She handed it to him. "Here, you wear it then." Strands of her hair clung to the teeth, gold in the morning sun.

He put it on and started waving, his hand high above his head.

"Not like that," Clara snapped. "You should never wave above the tiara."

Kara Pepin took it off Sam's head. "Like this?" she asked. She waved like the queen of England, her back straight, the tiara crooked. The tiara made its way from one person to the next. By the time it got to me, one of the corners had been broken off and it was missing two stones. I passed it on, not wanting to be the one holding it when we got to school.

Clara never looked away from the window, as if the newly planted fields were the most interesting thing she'd seen in all of her life.

Ruby picked up her sheers and lifted the hair. She had to cut three times. The first cut was below Clara's shoulders. Ruby gently laid the long rope of hair on the vanity. The second cut was above the shoulders and the third was even with Clara's earlobes. When the hair fell with the final cut, my mom, who'd sat beside me when Clara took the chair, gasped and grabbed my arm when we saw the finger marks that surrounded Clara's throat. I gripped her hand and held it hard. Later, I would see the half-moon bites my nails made on the back of my mom's hand.

We watched as Ruby shaped Clara's hair into a pixie cut. I knew that most of my friends would be demanding the same look within the week and I wondered if their mothers would ever again allow them to emulate the girl sitting in Ruby's chair.

When she finished, Ruby swept up most of the hair and removed the smock. Clara looked at herself in the mirror. We all watched as she realized that her desire to remove her long hair had not had the effect she'd needed. Clara thought her beauty had resided in her hair, that the hair was what drew people to her. With the smock gone, her neck was swan-like and, even with the angry marks left behind by a man who claimed to love her, she was more beautiful than when she walked in the door.

We waited as Ruby took Clara into the storage area. No one spoke or made eye contact the entire time they were in that dark space filled with hair dye and shampoos. I've always wondered if Clara denied what was happening to her. Did she defend him? Did she say anything at all?

When they came back out, she tried to pay. Ruby refused to take her money. "I feel like an artist today and you are my work of art."

Clara looked at the ground and mumbled "thank you." She stopped at the door and looked back. I could tell she wasn't seeing us. She waved, holding her hand at her shoulder and turning it from side to side, never lifting it above the imagined tiara.

No one spoke as the door closed, pushing a burst of hot hair back into the salon. My mother gathered her purse and paid Ruby. I glanced back at Mrs. Brubaker and Mrs. Collingsworth. Mrs. Brubaker had tears on her face that she didn't bother to wipe away.

My mom and I got back into the hot car instead of going to the restaurant. She drove us to the Tasty Freeze and got two Root Beer floats. We sat in the car, the air conditioning on high, and she told me about a man she'd dated after high school. How she'd loved him and how he had shoved her one night on his parents' front porch. How she stayed with him even though he made her feel less.

"It took a lot for me to walk away from him," she said, looking everywhere but at me.

"Why did you stay with him?" At fifteen, I still believed that life was made up of right and wrong, that answers were simple and concrete.

"I thought that I could make him see me. Care enough not to want to hurt me." Her face was red and she was trying not to cry. I wouldn't know the courage it took for her to tell me all she did until the first time I had to walk away from someone who had a tight hold on my heart. "I want more for you. I want you to first see yourself, love yourself, then you won't have to force others to see you and love you, they just will. Do you understand?"

I wanted to tell her that I'd already learned, just from watching, that there was always someone who wanted to tarnish beauty, make it as ugly as they felt inside. That there were those who took it upon themselves to keep others low, keep them in their designated place. I only nodded and tried not to picture Clara and the resigned look in her eyes, her hand held low, never raised above the tiara, waving goodbye.

ACKNOWLEDGEMENTS

There have been so many people who have supported me as I wrote and re-wrote these stories over the years. Words cannot convey the gratitude I feel for each and every one of you, but I will try.

For Regina, my first reader—your confidence when mine was weak carried me forward.

Becca—your optimism was contagious and kept me filled with hope.

A special thank you to Trey Penton and Emily Young at The Two Keys Press who championed these stories with enthusiasm and dedication. My deepest appreciation and admiration to you both.

Thank you to Clay Ramsey and Michael Varga for your encouragement, wise counsel and friendship.

Thank you to my siblings, aunts, uncles, nieces, nephews and cousins. We are an inimitable bunch, full of strong emotions and intractable determination. I couldn't have achieved this goal if I wasn't from such resilient and gritty stock.

I would like to acknowledge all of the remarkable people I've encountered throughout my life. Your strength, your determination to seek and grow, your willingness to be better and to do better is inspiring and thrilling to behold. Each of you has touched me, taught me, made me think, made me feel, and transformed me. My hope is that all of you have found some love, laughter and light in the time that we shared.

Finally, I would like to thank my mother, a fervent reader, who filled my early life with books. Even when we struggled to find common ground, we always had words to bridge the divide. Although she didn't get to see these stories in print, I believe with all my heart that she would be delighted.